TOP COW PRODUCTIONS PRESENTS

STAIRWAY

CREATED BY

MATT HAWKINS & RAFFAELE IENCO

PUBLISHED BY TOP COW PRODUCTIONS, INC.
LOS ANGELES

STAIRWAY, VOL. 1. First printing. August 2018. Published by Image Comics, Inc. Office of publicatio 2701 NW Vaughn St., Suite 780, Portland, OR 97210. ISBN: 978-1-5343-0801-5.

STAIRWAY

MATT HAWKINS
WRITER

RAFFAELE IENCO
ARTIST

TROY PETERI
LETTERER

"IF ANYONE HAS INSIGHT, LET HIM CALCULATE THE NUMBER OF THE BEAST, FOR IT IS THE NUMBER OF A MAN."

—REVELATION 13:18

CAST

DR. ALICIA VANDER

NICK CAMDEN

ETHAN CAMDEN

GREGORY HOPKINS

VINCENT MARTIN

Daily Note

MESSIAH_69

7/21/2048 23:23

The struggle continues. That bitch Janine Paul and the pathetic weak yes men she surrounds herself with are trying to tear me down again. Another investigation into our "research" by the NSF. I know she's just trying to hurt me for what I said about her during the election. Can't she just leave me be? She won for Christ's sake. Isn't being the President enough? Her vendetta is causing serious cost escalation. We're nearing a trillion dollars in capital outlay at this point. She'll kiss the ground I walk on when this is over. They all will. Thankfully I'm strong enough to do what needs to be done despite these petty bureaucrats. That's it for tonight, I'm tired. Hoping for some good visions tonight.

7/22/2048 03:38

Can't sleep, can't get those symbols out of my head. Only two pieces to go. R-65 and R-66 and it will be complete! It's definitely some form of sentience or artificial intelligence. It has been a long hard road. I can't wait!

7/22/2048 23:49

I've found some correlation between the symbols it emits and ancient texts. Definitely occult tie-ins, Crowley, Levay and Lovecraft seemed obsessed with this. The Bible, Kabbalah, the Qu'ran, gnostic gospels especially the Book of Enoch, looks like all these prophets were onto this same thing. These religious people are all so single-minded. I can sum religion up in one word: misinterpretation.

7/23/2048 02:23

Visions woke me up again. They can be terrifying, but after a few minutes I feel oddly calm. Like a general blissful feeling, I can't explain it. I saw a burning bush talking to a dirty bearded man in tattered robes, has to be Moses. A ghost-like hand writing on a sandstone wall in some ancient time. Should research that. I've wondered if it chose its form to show us it was not natural? Do they appear in nature? Have to look that up too.

7/24/2048 08:45

Taking a sleeping pill tonight, I've got to get some sleep. We were fined fifty million dollars today, but legal managed to stave off another raid pending some court maneuvers. These assholes want to make me look like a fool. Legal says I should do an apology tour on the Hill, that the good will is needed. I'll be goddamned before I apologize for trying to save the world.

CHAPTER 1

My name is
Gregory Hopkins.

I am waiving all
rights and speak of
my own free will.

This will be my formal
statement and recollection
of events before this
committee.

My intention is to tell you everything, regardless of
how distasteful some may find things I've done.
I want it all recorded and remembered, despite
possible self-incrimination.

There's nothing you can do to me
that's worse than the nightmares
plaguing me every night.

The device... the
event... they've changed
how I see humanity,
the world... everything.

I will accept the judgment of
this committee. I ask merely
that you recognize we've all
been given a second chance.

History may not
be kind to me.

I may be remembered
as worse than Hitler
and Stalin combined.

If that's how it has to be... so be it...
...someone had to do something.

WASHINGTON, DC 8/03/2023
THE FACES OF THE MILLIONS WHO ARE NOW GONE HAUNT ME...
...BUT I'D DO IT AGAIN.

YOU HAVE TO REMEMBER HOW BAD IT WAS BEFORE. HOW MANY WERE SUFFERING NEEDLESSLY.

THE NUCLEAR EXCHANGE BETWEEN INDIA AND PAKISTAN STARTED IT ALL.

Western India and Pakistan were irradiated wastelands after that.

China intervened while our president and Congress debated what to do.

Being sidelined hurt our national pride.

We were certainly front and center for the global economic collapse that followed.

The world was shit for over a decade and nothing anyone was doing made it any better.

That alone forced me to act.

I may not like how it happened and I'll live with what I've done, but it had to be.

The discovery in our DNA changed everything.
We don't know when nor do we know who or what did it...
...but someone or something seeded our DNA with information a long time ago that we were meant to find.
Whether this was done in our creation or infused into some progenitors of man...
...we may never know.

Dr. Alicia Vander can give you the detailed scientific explanations for the *"how"* of it all, it's out of my depth I'm afraid.
Despite her age now, she's quite gifted and remembers everything.
What I do know is it was given to us for a reason.

Someone or something wanted us to make this discovery and build it.
Was this God? Alien benefactors? Our ancestors or some lost human civilization?

They aren't here to tell us why.

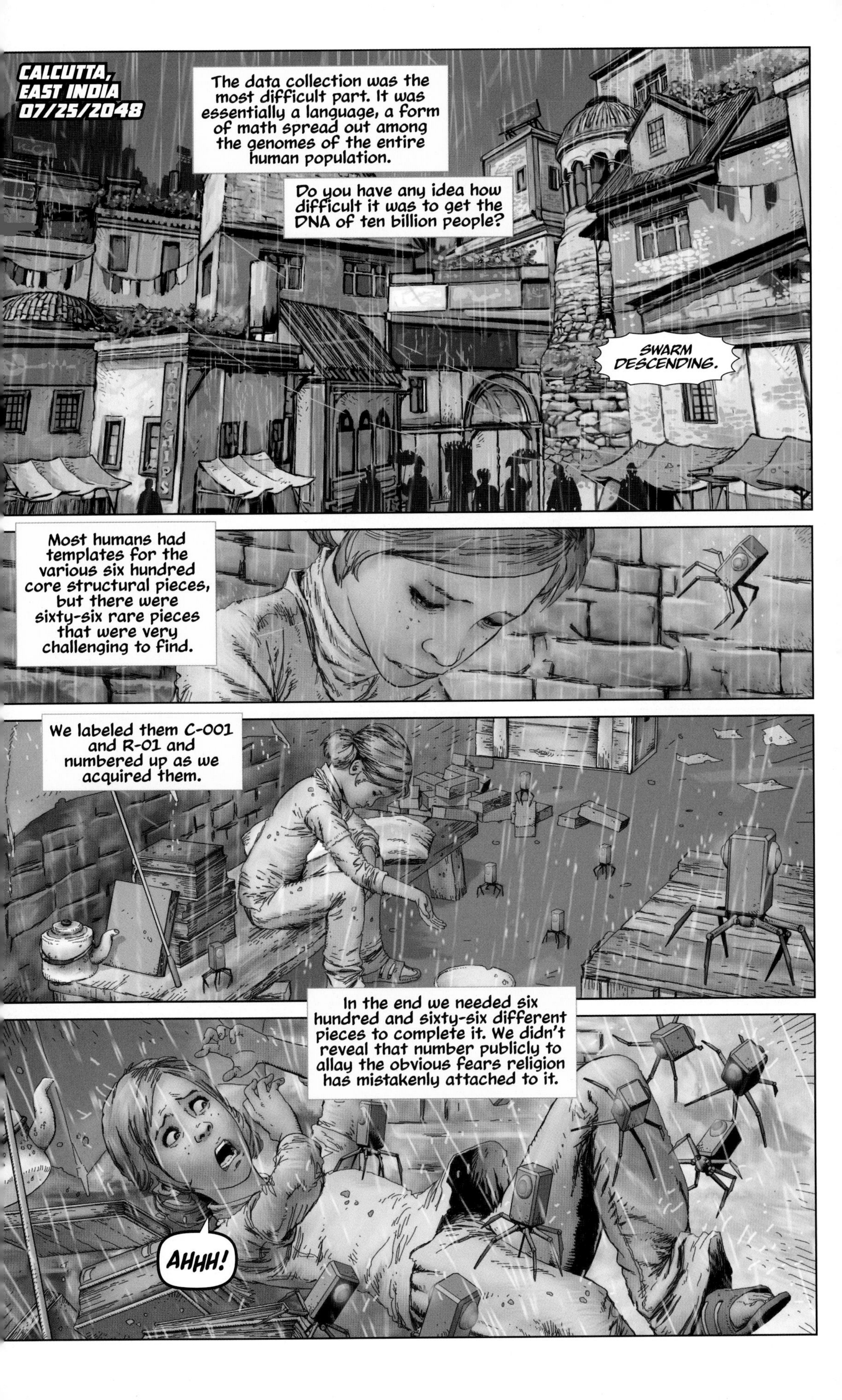
CALCUTTA, EAST INDIA 07/25/2048
The data collection was the most difficult part. It was essentially a language, a form of math spread out among the genomes of the entire human population.
Do you have any idea how difficult it was to get the DNA of ten billion people?
HOT CHIPS
SWARM DESCENDING.
Most humans had templates for the various six hundred core structural pieces, but there were sixty-six rare pieces that were very challenging to find.
We labeled them C-001 and R-01 and numbered up as we acquired them.
In the end we needed six hundred and sixty-six different pieces to complete it. We didn't reveal that number publicly to allay the obvious fears religion has mistakenly attached to it.
AHHH!

We took the R carriers into custody.
POSITIVE LOCATED IN BAGMARI. LOCKING COORDINATES.
The extraction process took a lot of time and we didn't know if we'd need them again.
TARGET TAGGED. ON THE MOVE. WE'RE IN PURSUIT.
WE DON'T HAVE PERMISSION HERE; LET'S MAKE THIS ONE QUICK.
ROGER THAT.
NO KILLING THIS TIME, ALPHA ONE.
ENTERING INDIAN AIRSPACE WITHOUT AUTHORIZATION IS TROUBLE. THEY'VE BEEN PUNCHY SINCE THE WAR.
WE'VE BEEN LOOKING FOR THESE LAST TWO PIECES FOR A YEAR NOW.
TAG AND BAG.
OMELETTES AND EGGS. IF THINGS GET BROKEN, THEN SO BE IT.
THE ENDS JUSTIFY THE MEANS.

AHHH!

Yes, that's correct...we kidnapped and unlawfully detained a bunch of civilians and some of them died.

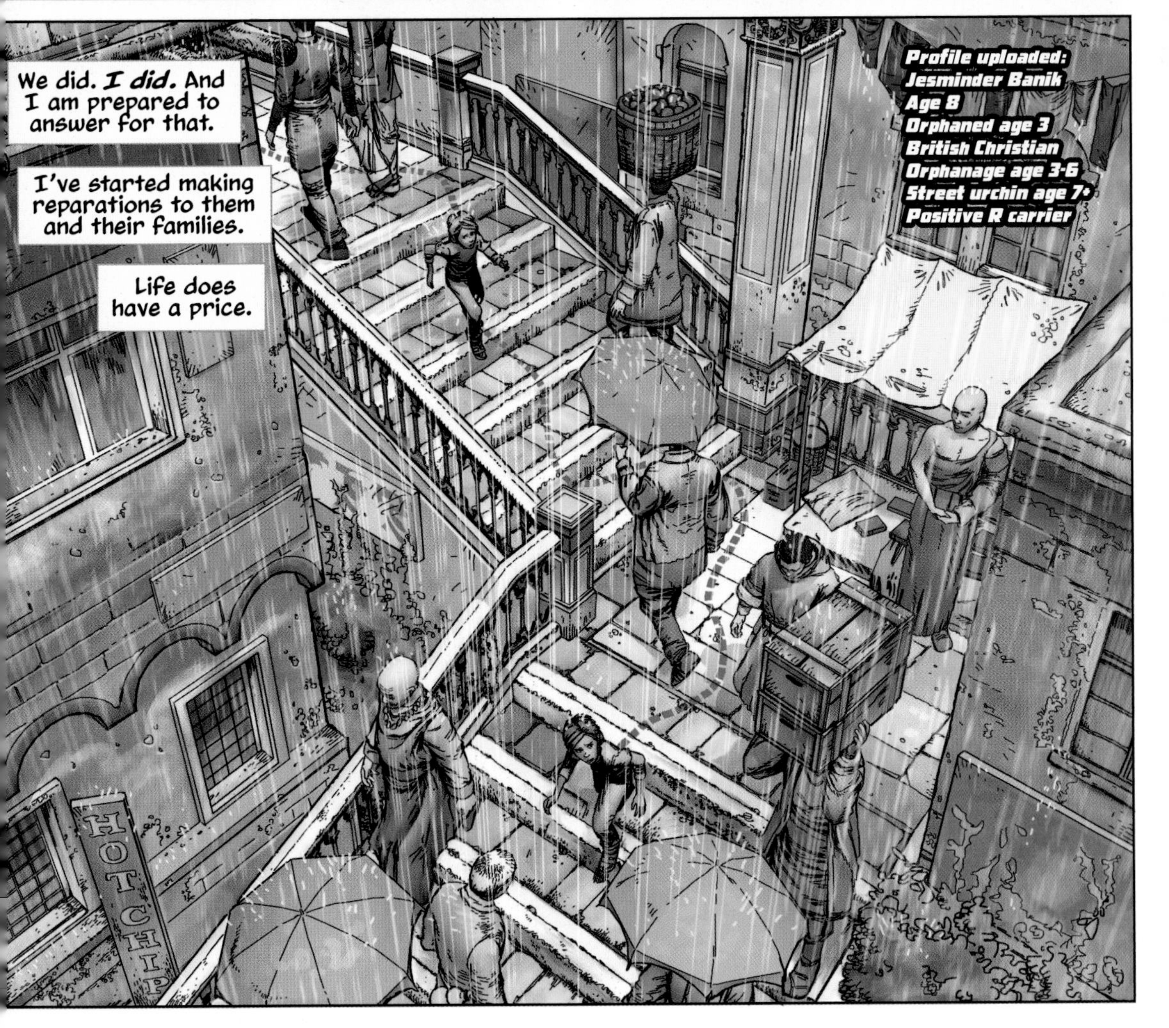
We did. *I did.* And I am prepared to answer for that.
I've started making reparations to them and their families.
Life does have a price.
Profile uploaded:
Jesminder Banik
Age 8
Orphaned age 3
British Christian
Orphanage age 3-6
Street urchin age 7+
Positive R carrier
HOT CHIP

INDIAN AIR FORCE INCOMING. ETA FOUR MINUTES.

‹JESMINDER, STOP. YOU HAVE TO COME WITH US.›*
‹LEAVE ME ALONE.›
*TRANSLATED FROM TAMIL.

‹NO!›

HERDING SUBJECT TOWARD YOUR POSITION, ALPHA ONE.

ROGER THAT.

JESMINDER, THAT'S YOUR NAME, YES, LOVE?
MY NAME'S VINCENT. I KNOW YOU SPEAK A LITTLE ENGLISH.

LOOK, DARLING, YOU'VE GOT US PEGGED WRONG. WE'RE NOT HERE TO HARM YOU. WE'RE HERE TO HELP. HAVEN'T YOU EVER WISHED FOR A BETTER LIFE?
YES, EVERY DAY. ALWAYS.

WE'RE GOING TO TAKE CARE OF YOU. YOU'LL NEVER HUNGER AGAIN. YOU'LL HAVE A FAMILY OF YOUR OWN IN AMERICA.

A FAMILY?

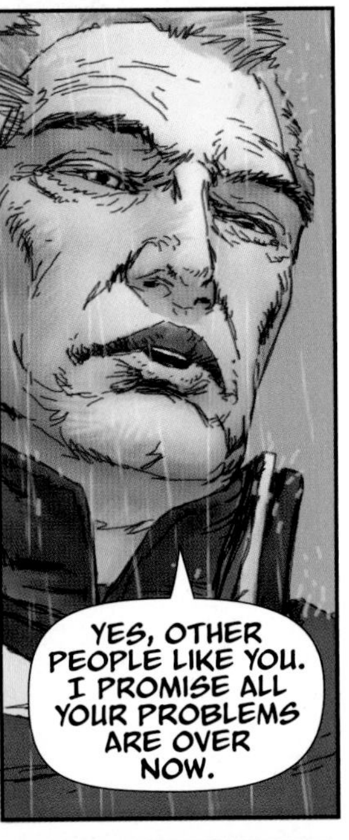
YES, OTHER PEOPLE LIKE YOU. I PROMISE ALL YOUR PROBLEMS ARE OVER NOW.

LET ME TAKE YOU WHERE YOU NEED TO BE.

I paid a high personal price as well. My son Peter was only twenty-three.
DISAPPOINTMENT. DO YOU KNOW WHAT THAT WORD MEANS? I'VE COME TO DESPISE THE WORD BECAUSE IT'S THE ONE WORD I MOST ASSOCIATE WITH YOU.
COUNTY HOLDING FACILITY

YOUR CHOICES PUNISH ME. YOU SPEND YOUR MONEY ON WHORES. DRUGS. IT'S LIKE YOUR LIFE MEANS NOTHING TO YOU.

YOU THINK IT'S EASY BEING YOUR SON? YOU DON'T KNOW--
SPARE ME THE SAD STORY ABOUT A RICH LOST BOY. I GAVE YOU EVERYTHING YOUR ENTIRE LIFE.

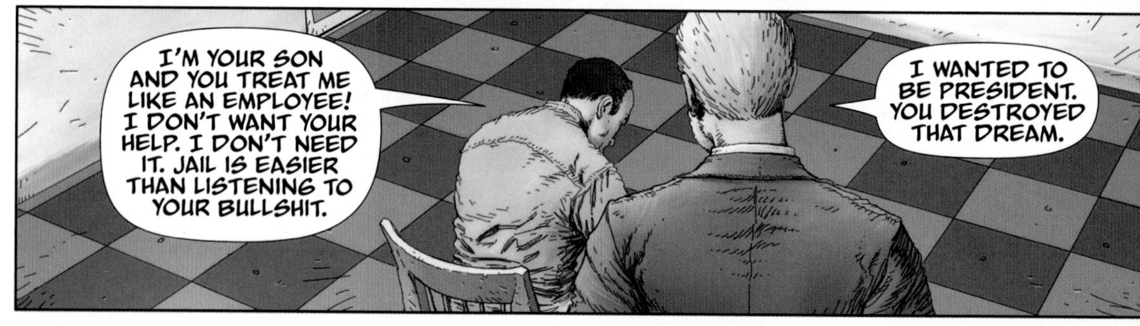
I'M YOUR SON AND YOU TREAT ME LIKE AN EMPLOYEE! I DON'T WANT YOUR HELP. I DON'T NEED IT. JAIL IS EASIER THAN LISTENING TO YOUR BULLSHIT.
I WANTED TO BE PRESIDENT. YOU DESTROYED THAT DREAM.

GOOD. YOU WOULD DESTROY THIS COUNTRY. YOU'RE A BAD PERSON, DAD. WHATEVER FLAWS I HAVE, I GOT FROM YOU.

IT WAS A MISTAKE TO HAVE YOU. YOU'RE MY ONLY FAILURE.

I did fail with my son.
POLICE
POLICE
POLICE

People need to earn something to truly respect it.

He was given everything and thus appreciated nothing.

Spare some change?
F$#% off.

Compassion kills you slowly. I learned that from raising him.

You really should talk to Dr. Vander.
DAD!

She made the initial discovery in her own DNA in grad school.
I SHOULD GO WITH THEM. ETHAN COULD USE SOME PEACEFUL MOM AND DAD TIME FOR A CHANGE.
I SEE THE PAIN IN HIS EYES...REMINDS ME OF MY OWN.

She decoded the information with an algorithm she wrote that we used for the entire program.
ALICIA!
I SHOULD GO, BUT I CAN'T. TOO MUCH TO DO FOR THE NEXT MILESTONE.

It was an overall schematic of the device and a blueprint for one piece...we know it now as R-01...the first of the sixty-six rare pieces.
WE'RE SO CLOSE AND THIS IS SO IMPORTANT...IF I KEEP SAYING THAT TO MYSELF I ALMOST BELIEVE IT.

She published one research paper before I bought her and took her off the grid.
WHO ARE YOU TALKING TO?

I was only able to hire her after destroying her credibility, though. Science can be a dirty business.
OH...OF COURSE. YOU'RE WORKING AND MUMBLING TO YOURSELF...AS ALWAYS.

I paid several leading scientists to discredit her work. She was young, the topic controversial.
IT'S SATURDAY, ALLY. WHY DON'T YOU COME WITH US?

The paper was retracted and her short science stardom faded into obscurity.
WE'RE AT A VERY CRUCIAL PHASE. OUR NEXT MILESTONE IS TUESDAY. IT'S IMPORTANT.
YOUR FAMILY'S NOT? OR DID YOU FORGET YOU HAVE ONE? THE JOB DESTROYED WHAT WE HAD, ALICIA. DON'T LOSE YOUR SON TOO.
THAT'S NOT FAIR, NICK. YOU LEFT. I DIDN'T MAKE YOU LEAVE.

YOU'RE MISSING YOUR CHILD'S LIFE. YOU DIDN'T HAVE TO LEAVE BECAUSE YOU'VE NEVER BEEN WITH US. I JUST REALIZED IT TOO LATE.

I'LL SEE YOU MONDAY. DON'T HAVE TOO MUCH FUN WITHOUT ME, OKAY?
I LOVE YOU, MOM. I KNOW WHAT YOU'RE DOING IS IMPORTANT.

RING RING

I manipulated her to achieve my goals...but I don't believe we'd have succeeded otherwise.
DR. VANDER.
WE'VE GOT A RARE POSITIVE INCOMING FROM INDIA. I'LL NEED YOU AT THE CORE FOR PROCESSING ASAP.

Dr. Vander is an undiagnosed autistic. A slight case, but enough to make her socially awkward and seemingly distant.

THE CORE
ROCKY MOUNTAINS, COLORADO
07/27/2048
9:15 AM
Her family was a distraction. I needed Nick out of the picture, but shouldering most of their childcare burden.

Consistent rumors of Alicia having affairs in the office played into her long hours and cold demeanor.
Come along, I want you to meet the nice man I've told you about.

I hired a woman to lure him away.
Welcome back, Vincent.

My methods, I know they sound terrible, but they worked.
You must be Jesminder. The photos don't do you justice.

Let's give you a tour of your new home.

ALICIA, I'D LIKE YOU TO MEET OUR NEW FRIEND.
HELLO, JESMINDER, MAY I CALL YOU JESSY FOR SHORT?

KAY.
YOU LOOK FRIGHTENED. OU CAN RELAX. KNOW WHAT 'S LIKE TO BE SCARED OF ADULTS.

I WON'T LET ANYTHING BAD HAPPEN TO YOU. I HAVE A SON ABOUT YOUR AGE.

licia was perfect for dealing with our ounger subjects. She was genuine, which nade them trust her.

Her profile showed a history of emotional abuse.
WHAT THE F$%K ARE YOU DOING?
YOU SAID I COULD DECORATE THE WALLS.

I MEANT WITH POSTERS, YOU IDIOT.
WORLD ECONOMIC COLLAPSE

CAN'T YOU BE NORMAL FOR ONCE?

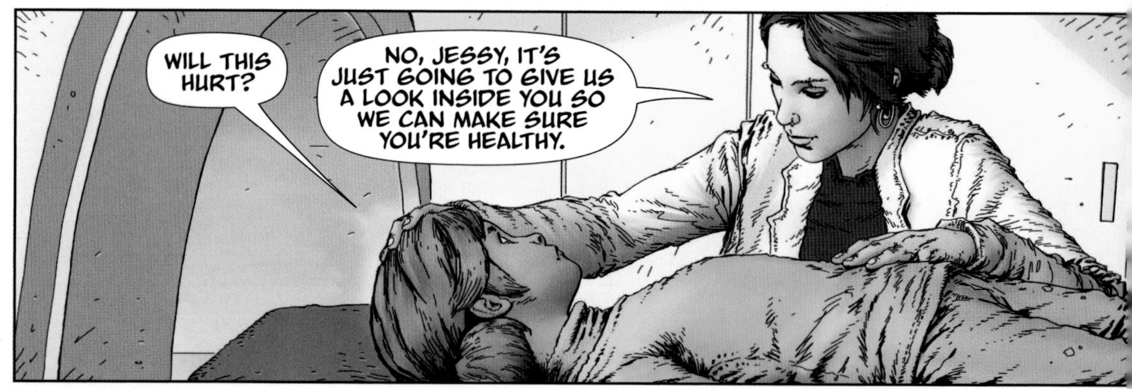
WILL THIS HURT?
NO, JESSY, IT'S JUST GOING TO GIVE US A LOOK INSIDE YOU SO WE CAN MAKE SURE YOU'RE HEALTHY.

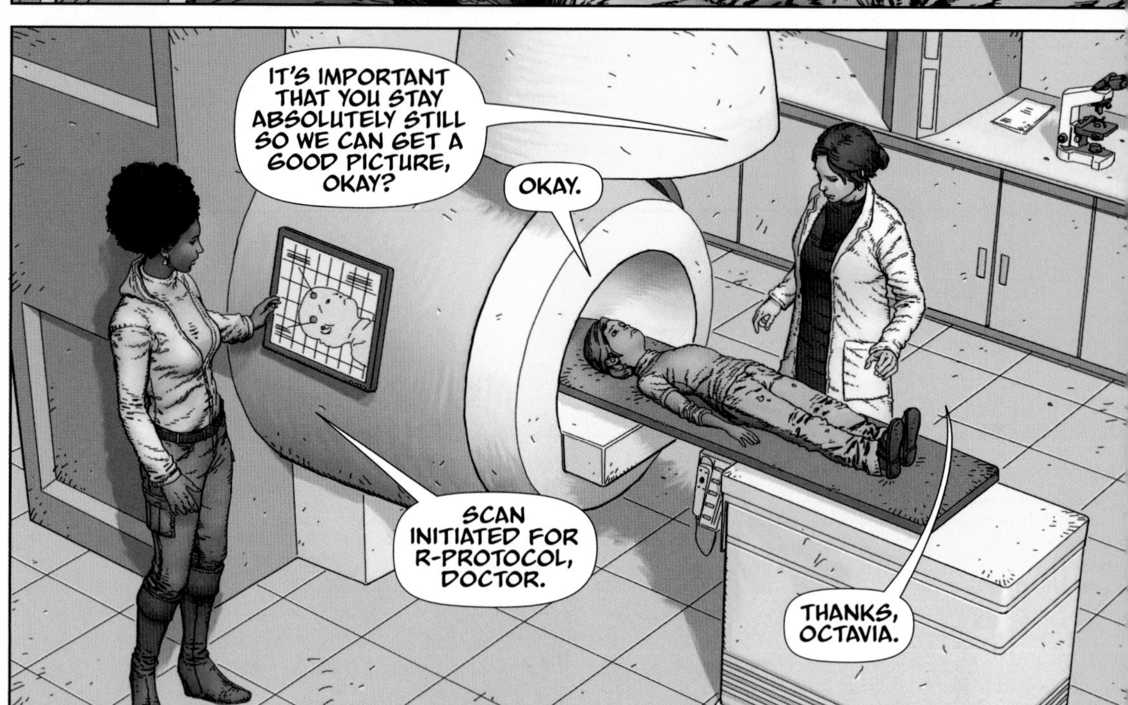
IT'S IMPORTANT THAT YOU STAY ABSOLUTELY STILL SO WE CAN GET A GOOD PICTURE, OKAY?
OKAY.
SCAN INITIATED FOR R-PROTOCOL, DOCTOR.
THANKS, OCTAVIA.

CONFIRMATION OF R-CARRIER. MATCHES THE FIELD ASSESSMENT.
DECRYPTING HER DNA NOW.

IT'S A NEW PIECE. DESIGNATE R-65. LET'S PRINT IT OUT.
THAT JUST LEAVES ONE MORE, HOW EXCITING!

THAT PART OF INDIA WAS THE LAST UNMAPPED GRID ON THE PLANET. DO YOU THINK WE'LL FIND THE LAST PIECE?
YES, WE WERE MEANT TO BUILD IT.

WHAT DO YOU THINK THE MACHINE DOES?
I DON'T KNOW. I'VE NOT HAD ACCESS TO IT. HOPKINS KEEPS ME ON THE DATA RETRIEVAL TEAM.

YOU OKAY NOW, SWEETIE? YOU WANT TO GET SOMETHING TO EAT?
I AM HUNGRY.

WELL, WE HAVE A WHOLE BUNCH OF TASTY TREATS JUST FOR YOU.

IT'S R-65.
EXCELLENT WORK AS ALWAYS, DR. VANDER.
I'LL TAKE THAT.

I WANT TO SEE IT.
THIS AGAIN? THIS PROJECT WILL CHANGE THE COURSE OF HUMAN HISTORY. IT MAKES THE MANHATTAN PROJECT LOOK LIKE A QUAINT LITTLE TEA PARTY.
I'VE SPENT OVER NINE HUNDRED BILLION DOLLARS OF MY OWN MONEY TO BUILD THIS THING AND KEEP IT QUIET--

YOU KNOW WHAT IT DOES, DON'T YOU? IT WOULDN'T EXIST WITHOUT ME.
YOU'RE RIGHT, MY DEAR.

I needed to bring her in. We'd scanned every living human, dug up every corpse, hacked one hundred fifty years of COTUS data and acquired every company with a DNA database.
We could not find R-66, the final piece of the greatest puzzle in history.

PERHAPS IT IS TIME TO BRING YOU UP TO SPEED. GIVEN SOME OF YOUR FAMILY DRAMA I WASN'T SURE IF YOU WERE FULLY COMMITTED TO THE PROJECT.
SO I ASK YOU BEFORE PANDORA'S BOX IS FULLY OPENED TO YOU...ARE YOU COMMITTED?

YOU KNOW I AM.

THIS ROOM...IS MASSIVE.
I CALL IT THE VAULT.
SEEMED APROPOS NOW THAT IT HOLDS EARTH'S MOST VALUABLE POSSESSION.
WE'RE SIX HUNDRED FEET BELOW GROUND HERE. THERE'S NOT ANOTHER HUMAN BEING FOR FORTY MILES THAT DOESN'T WORK FOR ME.

YOU'RE NOW ONE OF ONLY THREE PEOPLE WHO'VE SEEN IT UP CLOSE.

IT CAME ALIVE, FOR LACK OF A BETTER WAY OF SAYING IT, AFTER THE SIX HUNDRED CORE PIECES WERE COMBINED.

AND I NEED TO REMIND YOU OF THE CONFIDENTIAL NATURE OF ANYTHING YOU SEE OR FEEL HERE.
FEEL?

YES...IT COMMUNICATES WITH VISIONS. BOTH VINCENT AND I'VE SEEN...FELT... A LOT.

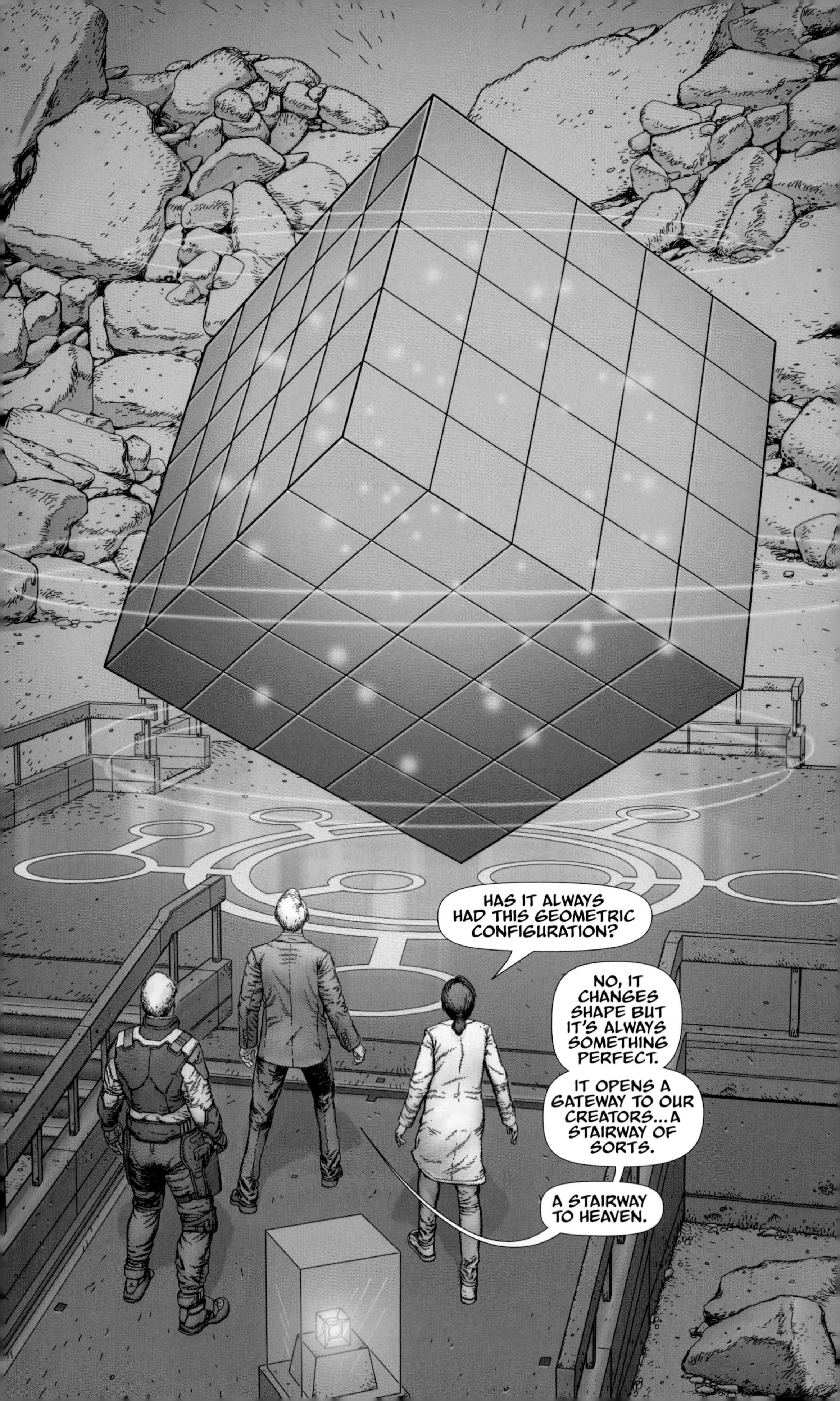
HAS IT ALWAYS HAD THIS GEOMETRIC CONFIGURATION?
NO, IT CHANGES SHAPE BUT IT'S ALWAYS SOMETHING PERFECT.
IT OPENS A GATEWAY TO OUR CREATORS...A STAIRWAY OF SORTS.
A STAIRWAY TO HEAVEN.

THIS NEW PIECE...IT'S VIBRATING.

KRAK

CRASH

HAVE YOU SEEN THIS BEFORE?
YES, BUT INTEGRATION HAS BECOME MORE AGGRESSIVE AS IT NEARS COMPLETION.

I DO FEEL IT.

THAT'S LANGUAGE...WE NEED TO WRITE THIS DOWN.
I HAVE CAMERAS RECORDING IT TWENTY-FOUR SEVEN.

HAVE SYMBOLS APPEARED BEFORE?
YES, BUT THE SEQUENCE OF SHAPES EXPANDS AS NEW PIECES ARE ADDED. IT BROADCASTS A SIGNAL IN THE PETAHERTZ RANGE. I'VE RESPONDED ON THE SAME FREQUENCY WITH A HANDHELD DEVICE WE'VE MADE, BUT SO FAR IT HAS NOT RESPONDED.
THE VISIONS...WHAT ELSE HAVE THEY SHOWN YOU?

I knew the truth would derail her, so I had to lie.
JUST THE STAIRWAY LEADING TO THE OTHER SIDE. THE BEINGS THERE ARE COMPOSED OF ENERGY...LIGHT.
I DON'T KNOW HOW TO DESCRIBE THEM OTHER THAN ANGELS. VINCENT AND I'VE BOTH SEEN THE SAME THING.

DO YOU UNDERSTAND NOW WHY WE KEEP A LID ON ALL THIS? THE WORLD IS ALREADY A SHITHOLE, WE DON'T NEED ANOTHER RELIGIOUS WAR.
THAT IT HAS THE "MARK OF THE BEAST" NUMBER OF PIECES ALONE WILL FREAK OUT THE ZEALOTS.

07/27/2048
16:21
RING
RING

HEY, ALLY. THANKS FOR CALLING ME BACK. I WANTED TO APOLOGIZE FOR LAYING INTO YOU IN FRONT OF ETHAN. WE'VE HAD A BUSY DAY.

HE'S ASLEEP HERE IN THE CAR NOW, SNORING AWAY, SO SPEAK FREELY.

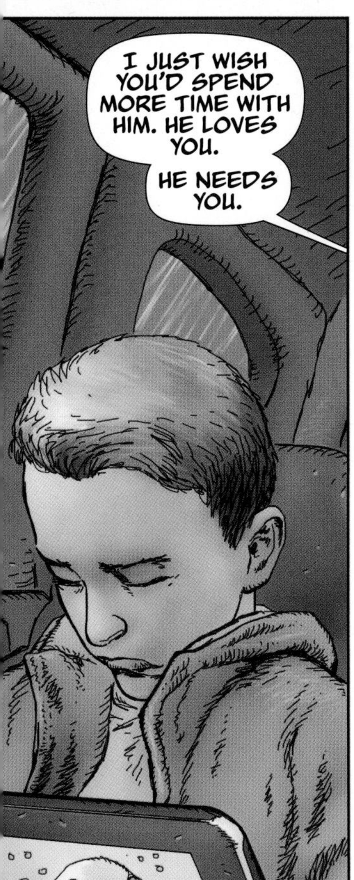
I JUST WISH YOU'D SPEND MORE TIME WITH HIM. HE LOVES YOU.
HE NEEDS YOU.

NICK... WE ARE SO CLOSE TO FINISHING THIS, I CAN'T TELL YOU MUCH ABOUT IT... BUT IT'S GOING TO CHANGE EVERYTHING.
ALICIA

YOU SAID ALMOST THE EXACT SAME THING FIVE YEARS AGO.

YOU SAID ALMOST THE EXACT SAME THING FIVE YEARS AGO.
WE HAVE TO STOP HIM FROM DISTRACTING HER WITH THIS INANE NONSENSE.

STRENGTHEN HER FOCUS.
DO WE EVEN HAVE TIME FOR THIS WITH THE GOVERNMENT UP OUR ASS?

ANY MORE DRAMA AND THEY MIGHT SHUT US DOWN FOR GOOD. IT'S TAKING ALL OF LEGAL'S TIME TO KEEP THEM FROM RAIDING THIS PLACE.

WE NEED HER HELP TO FIND OR CREATE R-66 OR ALL THIS WAS FOR NOTHING. SHE'S LINKED TO THE CUBE, HAS BEEN SINCE THE BEGINNING.
HER DNA, THE DNA OF THE OTHER RARE CARRIERS. THEY'RE ALL RELATED TO WITHIN TEN GENERATIONS.

TAKE CARE OF IT.

HEY, SLEEPYHEAD, I SPOKE TO YOUR MOM EARLIER. SHE'S GOING TO TRY AND MEET US FOR BREAKFAST TOMORROW.

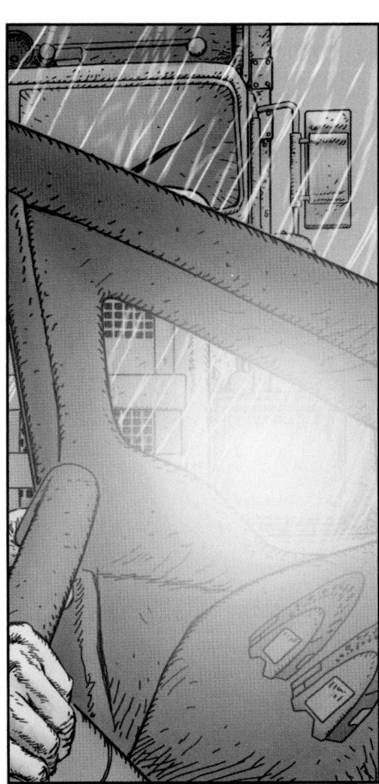

MESSIAH_69

Daily Note

7/25/2048 23:56

Dr. Vander is becoming increasingly difficult to manage. Reviewing her surveillance report has shown a distinct lack of focus. She spent two hours the other night going through her son's baby photos. That's not acceptable at this pivotal moment. Nothing can distract us from finding this last piece and finishing this. CHRIST! Why am I burdened this way? Why am I the only one that can do this? Vincent is the only one I absolutely trust and still I keep evidence to put him away forever if need be.

7/28/2048 21:19

Insanely busy last couple of days. We've gone back over the DNA databases…all of them…and nothing on the last piece. The neo-natal samples have all come back negative. I've started combing occult and religious texts looking for anything that might help give us a clue of sorts. I'm convinced these so-called prophets of the past were able to access the cube by some other means. How?!?!? I'm getting increasingly desperate. I've had to retain every law firm in Washington so they can't be used to litigate against me.

7/29/2048 03:02

Visions of the earth remade. Glorious! I feel inspired. I can't let anything get in the way of finishing this. Dr. Vander is the key. I have to figure out a way to motivate her. Hmm when she's had emotional pain in the past she buried herself in her work. Maybe it's time to get serious.

Genetics sent me a report today that her DNA and the DNA of her banked umbilical cord blood and R-01 WAS NOT THERE. So she was NOT born with it. Is it possible it's an epigenetic change? Did someone add it via gene editing? How? This has opened a whole new line of questions we have no answers to. Reminder to open an investigation into her parents' birth DNA. They didn't bank baby blood, no one did back then, but can't hurt to try.

7/30/2048 00:18

Damn it! Am I the only one that can do anything right? The world is lucky the cube found me. I'll be a benevolent dictator. Democracy is for the weak. Why would you give an uninformed moron an equal vote to a great mind? Plutocracy is better than democracy but a benevolent dictatorship by a supreme mind would be the best of all. I will save them despite themselves.

8/02/2048 22:47

Why is it a cube? Found this on a website: "The cube is a three-dimensional square; it is a symbol of stability and permanence, of geometric perfection. It represents the final stage of a cycle of immobility, it can be seen as the truth, because it looks the same from any perspective, it is commonly thought of as the counterpart of the sphere. The cube is, in essence, the squaring of a circle. Scientifically, the cube usually represents salt. It is the earth: a square plus the four elements plus three dimensions. Frequently forms allegories with solidity and the persistence of virtues, hence its relation to thrones or chariots." More religious nonsense, sigh…wish I could trust more people to help with analysis.

CHAPTER 2
RAFF
IENCO

I didn't want this responsibility, but the Cube chose *me*.
I was destined to be its prophet for this age.
When I finally got up the nerve to touch it, it revealed its purpose to me. All prophets are seen as dangerous. Insane. Monstrous.
But do not doubt mankind stared at the possibility of its extinction.
Can you blame me for saving our species?

During the Indian/Pakistani war, thirty-five nuclear blasts were detonated in less than an hour.

Hundreds of thousands of square kilometers of irradiated wasteland was the immediate result, but the longer term environmental effects were catastrophic worldwide.

Maps had been rewritten in ways thousands of years of conventional war never could.

I traveled the world to see how I might be able to help as a private citizen.

Miami, New York, Los Angeles...all underwater. And we had it good compared to the rest of the world... our seas held some hope of life.

There were millions of homeless...refugees... in our own country.

Starving. They needed help.
THESE PEOPLE DISGUST ME.

I had a moral obligation to help others less fortunate than myself.

I ran for president and lost. The world wasn't ready for true leadership. And I watched while we pranced to our own destruction.
WANT TO GET HIGH! PLEASE GIVE ME MONEY!

The ice caps were almost gone.

I searched the world for answers.
Some way to save us from ourselves.

While the rest of the world fought over shrinking scraps.

There was so much death...everywhere...
I activated the device because I knew it was our only salvation.
You can call me evil.

Call me whatever you want, but I saw the world for what it is and knew drastic measures had to be taken.

I took this burden upon myself. How could I not act when I knew I was the only one who would?
The alternative was oblivion.

And did I actually kill anyone?
DENVER, CO
07/27/2048
19:02
MARTIN MEMORIAL

THIRD DOOR TO THE LEFT.

ETHAN? NICK?

OH MY GOD! MY BABY.
HE'S GOING TO BE OKAY. THEY KNOCKED HIM OUT.

MY SWEET BOY, I'M SO SORRY I WASN'T THERE.
ALLY... CAN WE TALK OUTSIDE?

THE DOCTOR WILL BE BACK IN ABOUT A HALF HOUR IF YOU WANT TO SPEAK TO HIM.
OKAY... THANK YOU, NURSE.

IT WASN'T MY FAULT. THAT TRUCK BROADSIDED ME.
I DIDN'T SAY IT WAS YOUR FAULT.
I'M SORRY... I JUST FEEL SO MUCH GUILT ABOUT EVERY-THING. ETHAN... MY AFFAIR.

I DON'T BLAME YOU. I'M NOT THE KIND OF WOMAN A MAN LIKE YOU NEEDS.
I PRETENDED I COULD BE.

I STILL LOVE YOU, ALLY.
DID YOU EVER LOVE ME?
I...I DON'T KNOW.

I'M NOT SURE I KNOW HOW.

I'M SORRY.

Of everything I did, what happened to Dr. Vander's son haunts me the most. "Suffer the little children who come unto me." God bears the weight of tragedy. I needed to do the same.
Grief provided her focus. It strengthened her work.
That doesn't excuse what I did, but the results were undeniable.
I LOVE YOU MOMMY! ETHAN

The visions from the cube changed with Alicia's inclusion.
IT'S SHOWING US HOW TO ACTIVATE IT.

They took a more theological turn...dark. It was both exhilarating and terrifying.
WE MUST BE CLOSE TO FINDING THE FINAL PIECE.

I AM THE ALPHA AND THE OMEGA.

WHAT DO YOU WANT?

I AM MAKING EVERYTHING NEW.
I AM THE BEGINNING AND THE END.

I'M SCARED.
THIS IS A GOOD THING. I NOW KNOW THE SEQUENCE TO ACTIVATE, WE JUST NEED TO FIND THAT LAST PIECE.

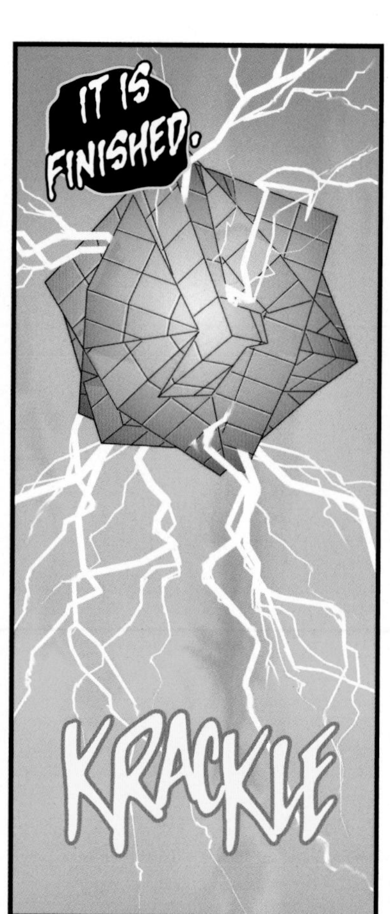
IT IS FINISHED.
KRACKLE

KRAKATHOOM

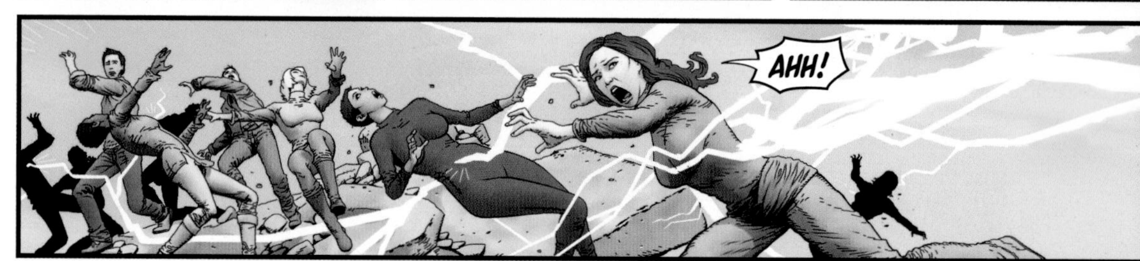
AHH!

Those last visions reminded me of Oppenheimer's quote from the Bhagavad Gita.
"Now I am become death.
"The destroyer of worlds."

All religious texts have destruction and rebirth in there somewhere.
Mankind embraced religion because it never understood the purpose of death.

MOMMY!

ETHAN?! WHAT ARE YOU DOING HERE?

A SACRIFICE IS REQUIRED.
KRAK
AHH!

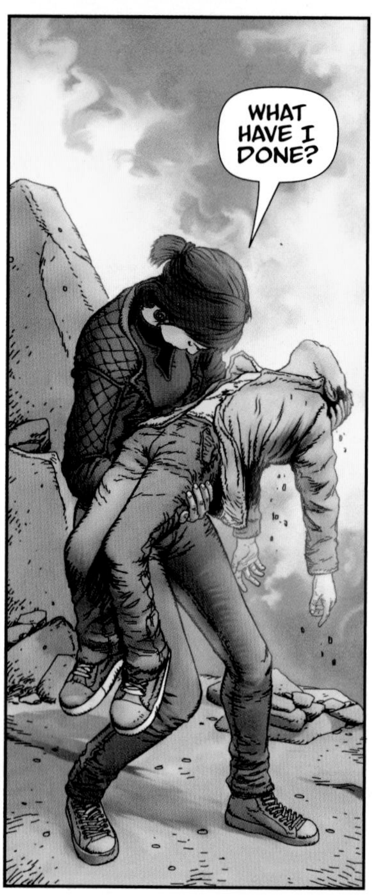
WHAT HAVE I DONE?

NO, NO! ETHAN!

NO!

Despite the apocalyptic visions, the fear they instilled didn't stay long after waking up...an odd calmness would descend...almost like the effect of a drug kicking in...

Ethan's awake and keeps talking about some cube. He wants to see you.

...or the acceptance of something inevitable.

If anything, the visions made me feel like I was connected to everyone and everything. It's hard to explain.
ARTIN MEMORIAL

WHOA...TAKE IT EASY, HE'S FINE. HE'S ASLEEP AGAIN.
DOCTORS ARE HAPPY WITH HIS PROGRESS.
WHAT DID HE SAY ABOUT THE CUBE?

NOTHING THAT MADE SENSE, I FIGURED IT WAS THE PAIN MEDS TALKING.

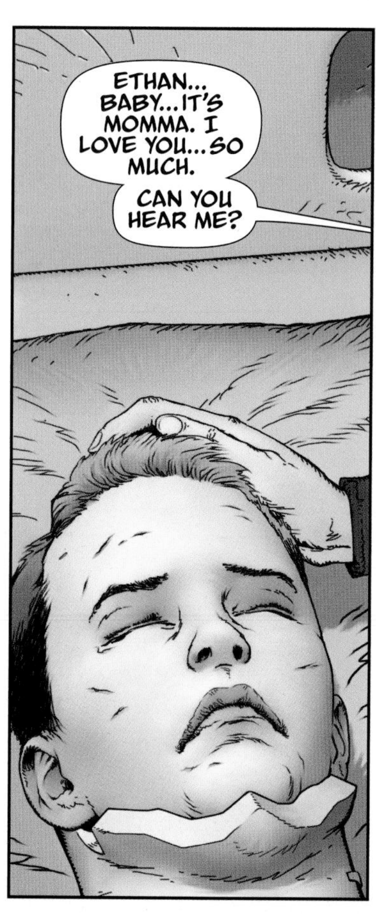
ETHAN... BABY...IT'S MOMMA. I LOVE YOU...SO MUCH.
CAN YOU HEAR ME?

MOMMY?
YEAH, BABY, I'M HERE. HOW ARE YOU FEELING?

OKAY, I GUESS. JUST SO TIRED... HAVING WEIRD DREAMS.

DOCTOR SAID TO LET HIM SLEEP AS MUCH AS HE CAN. HE'S HEALING UP WELL.
THANK YOU, NICK.

I'M SO SORRY...FOR EVERYTHING.

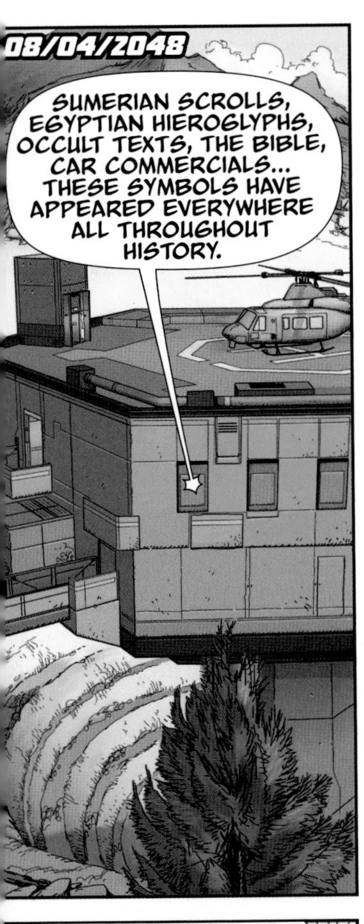
08/04/2048
SUMERIAN SCROLLS, EGYPTIAN HIEROGLYPHS, OCCULT TEXTS, THE BIBLE, CAR COMMERCIALS... THESE SYMBOLS HAVE APPEARED EVERYWHERE ALL THROUGHOUT HISTORY.

TWO ENGLISHMEN IN THE 16TH CENTURY GOT FURTHER THAN ANYONE ELSE. A MATHEMATICIAN NAMED JOHN DEE AND SPIRIT MEDIUM EDWARD KELLEY. THEY REFERRED TO IT AS CELESTIAL SPEAK, BUT LATER IT WAS CALLED ENOCHIAN.
THEY THOUGHT IT WAS THE LANGUAGE OF ANGELS.
DO YOU REALLY BELIEVE THERE ARE ANGELS ON THE OTHER SIDE OF THE STAIRWAY?
ANGELS... EVOLVED HUMANS... OTHER FORMS OF LIFE...WHO KNOWS?
THE DOGMA OF RELIGION AND THE ARROGANCE OF SCIENCE HAVE BEEN WAGING A FUTILE BATTLE SINCE THE BEGINNING.

THAT THEY MAY HAVE TOLD THE SAME STORY FROM TWO DIFFERENT PERSPECTIVES IS THE ULTIMATE IRONY OF HUMAN HISTORY.
HOW WERE EARLIER CULTURES ABLE TO ACCESS IT WITHOUT THE DNA SCIENCE?

REPORTS OF SUPERNATURAL PHENOMENA... I'VE WONDERED IF THEY MIGHT BE THE CODE TRYING TO COMMUNICATE WITH US.
THERE HAS TO BE MORE THAN ONE WAY TO REACH THIS CONSCIOUSNESS.

YOU, VINCENT AND I'VE SHARED VISIONS. WE LOOK AT IT AS A FORM OF TECHNOLOGY, PERHAPS AN ARTIFICIAL INTELLIGENCE SPEAKING TO US... BUT LESS ADVANCED PEOPLE WOULD HAVE MISTAKEN THIS AS SPIRITUAL.

THE CONCEPT OF AN AFTERLIFE ORIGINATED BECAUSE OUR ANCESTORS DREAMED OF LOVED ONES THAT HAD DIED...AND THEY ASSUMED THIS MEANT THEY STILL EXISTED SOMEWHERE.
LET ME ASK STRAIGHT UP: DO YOU BELIEVE IN GOD?
ANY GOD THAT WOULD CREATE THIS WORLD ISN'T WORTHY OF WORSHIP.

WHAT DO YOU BELIEVE?
I ACCEPT THE POSSIBILITY OF AN OLD TESTAMENT GOD...
KILLS INDISCRIMINATELY, JUST LIKE NATURE. MAKES MORE SENSE.

I MIGHT NOT BELIEVE IN GOD, BUT I HATE HIM A LITTLE.
I HATE ANYTHING THAT WOULD LET MY SON ETHAN --
DR. VANDER, COME WITH ME.

IT'S NOT GOD WE HAVE TO WORRY ABOUT IT'S US.

CAN YOU IMAGINE THE CUBE IN THE HANDS OF OUR GOVERNMENT? A FOREIGN GOVERNMENT?

I'VE BEEN HAVING THESE VISIONS FOR YEARS NOW, THEY TAP INTO YOUR OWN PRIMAL FEARS AND DESIRES. IT'S A TEST OF SOME KIND.
THESE BEINGS ON THE OTHER SIDE COULD TEACH US SO MUCH...OR THEY COULD DEEM US UNWORTHY AND WIPE US OUT.

THE GOVERNMENT IS TRYING TO SHUT ME DOWN. I CAN HOLD THEM OFF FOR A FEW MORE DAYS AT MOST.

WHO WOULD YOU PREFER MAKE FIRST CONTACT? US? OR SOME SPECIAL FORCES TEAM?

WE NEED TO GO PUBLIC. THAT CONFUSION MAY BUY US A FEW MORE DAYS TO FIND THE LAST PIECE.
WE'RE SO CLOSE TO FINISHING WHAT YOU AND I HAVE SACRIFICED TEN YEARS OF OUR LIVES FOR.

I ADMIRE YOU, DR. VANDER... ALICIA.

I'VE ALWAYS THOUGHT OF YOU AS THE DAUGHTER I NEVER HAD.
ARE YOU WITH ME?

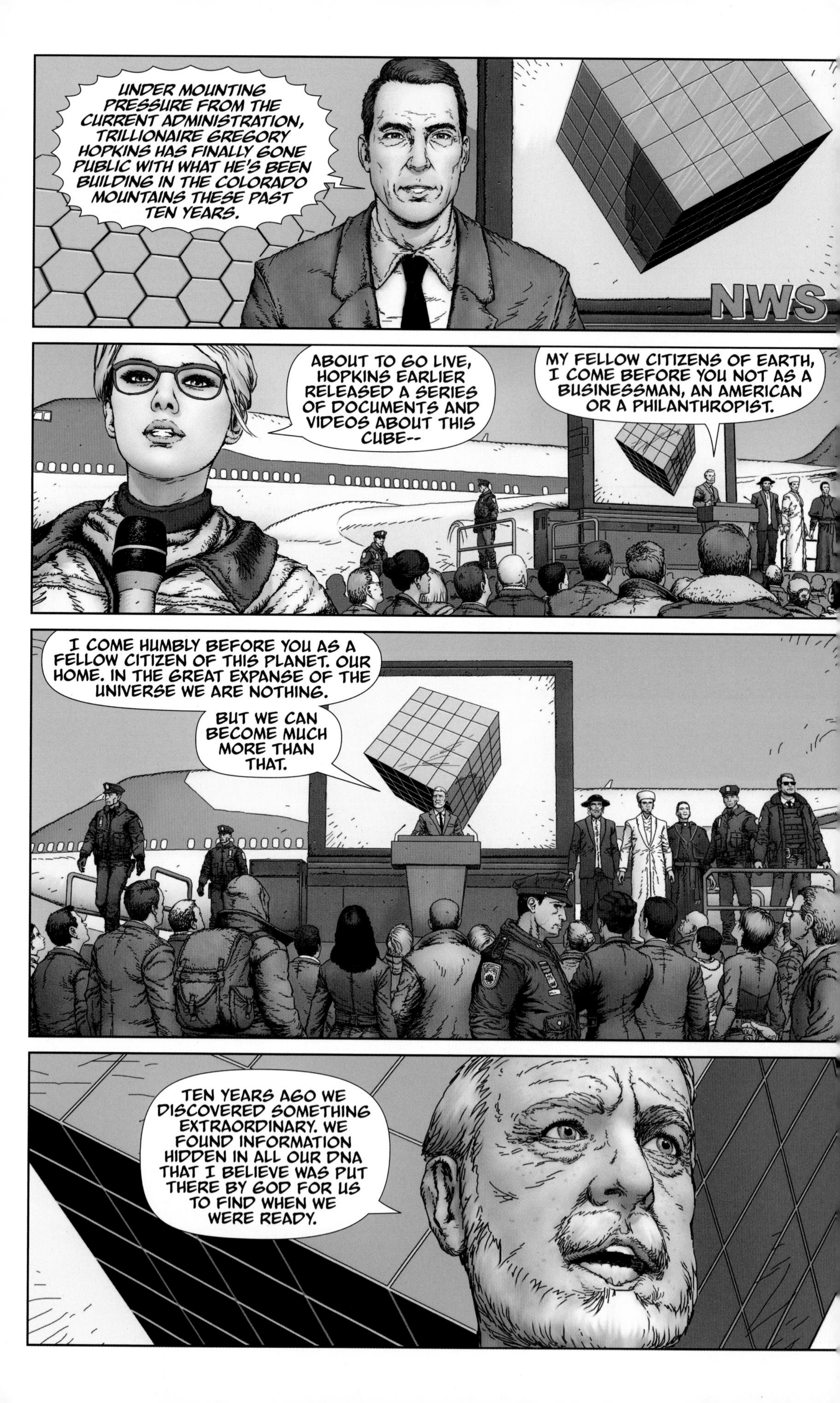
UNDER MOUNTING PRESSURE FROM THE CURRENT ADMINISTRATION, TRILLIONAIRE GREGORY HOPKINS HAS FINALLY GONE PUBLIC WITH WHAT HE'S BEEN BUILDING IN THE COLORADO MOUNTAINS THESE PAST TEN YEARS.
NWS
ABOUT TO GO LIVE, HOPKINS EARLIER RELEASED A SERIES OF DOCUMENTS AND VIDEOS ABOUT THIS CUBE--
MY FELLOW CITIZENS OF EARTH, I COME BEFORE YOU NOT AS A BUSINESSMAN, AN AMERICAN OR A PHILANTHROPIST.
I COME HUMBLY BEFORE YOU AS A FELLOW CITIZEN OF THIS PLANET. OUR HOME. IN THE GREAT EXPANSE OF THE UNIVERSE WE ARE NOTHING.
BUT WE CAN BECOME MUCH MORE THAN THAT.
TEN YEARS AGO WE DISCOVERED SOMETHING EXTRAORDINARY. WE FOUND INFORMATION HIDDEN IN ALL OUR DNA THAT I BELIEVE WAS PUT THERE BY GOD FOR US TO FIND WHEN WE WERE READY.

THIS DATA ONCE DECODED FORMED SCHEMATICS AND BLUEPRINTS FOR A HOST OF INCREDIBLE MACHINES, INCLUDING THE CUBE YOU NOW SEE.

THIS CUBE OPENS A GATEWAY...A DOOR TO ANOTHER WORLD... I LIKE TO CALL IT A "STAIRWAY TO HEAVEN" AFTER A SONG MY FATHER LOVED SO MUCH.

When I said all this... I thought it was a bunch of religious nonsense to placate the simpletons... now I'm not so sure.
I RESPECT ALL FAITHS. WE ARE ALL PEOPLE OF THE BOOK.

THE CUBE IS SENTIENT, IT HAS COMMUNICATED WITH US AND RELAYED HOW IT WANTS TO HELP US ACHIEVE OUR NEXT STEP IN SPIRITUAL DEVELOPMENT.

WE CAN END POVERTY, WAR, HUNGER, DISEASE AND BECOME WHAT WE WERE DESTINED TO BE. WE CAN UNLOCK OUR OWN HIDDEN POWER. IF WE HAVE THE COURAGE.

PASTOR MARKHAM, YOU'VE COME OUT VOCALLY SUPPORTING HOPKINS DESPITE YOUR HEAVY CRITICISM OF HIM DURING HIS PRESIDENTIAL RUN.

YES, MARY, I'VE SPOKEN TO GREGORY HOPKINS. HE'S A CHANGED MAN. I THANK THE LORD FOR SHOWING HIM THE LIGHT.

IT'S SCARY BUT IT MAKES SENSE, YA KNOW? I NEVER KNEW APOCALYPSE MEANT TO DISCLOSE A HIDDEN TRUTH.
SURE MAKES THE END TIMES LESS SCARY, SORRY, HOLLYWOOD.

IT'S ALL SO EXCITING, I WANT TO GO.

I DON'T BUY IT, GUY'S A CROOK AND ALWAYS HAS BEEN. GOVERNMENT SHOULD TAKE THAT OVER BEFORE HE KILLS US ALL.

MR. HOPKINS, ANY FINAL WORD TO SILENCE YOUR CRITICS?
I SPOKE WITH THE PRESIDENT AND ASSURED HER WE WOULD DO NOTHING UNTIL HER TEAM ARRIVES TO OVERSEE COMPLETION.
I WOULD NEVER ACTIVATE SUCH A DEVICE WITHOUT THE FULL SUPPORT OF THE WORLD.

I was not certain Dr. Vander was with me.
YOU SAY ONE THING AND DO ANOTHER.

WHY WOULD ANYONE TRUST YOU?
Gregory Hopkins
Hopkins Corp

So I engineered a test of loyalty.

She failed.

WHAT THE...?

THESE ARE...ISOLATION CELLS?

JESSY!

HELP ME, PLEASE.
I'M GOING TO GET YOU OUT.

I'M SO SORRY. I DIDN'T KNOW.

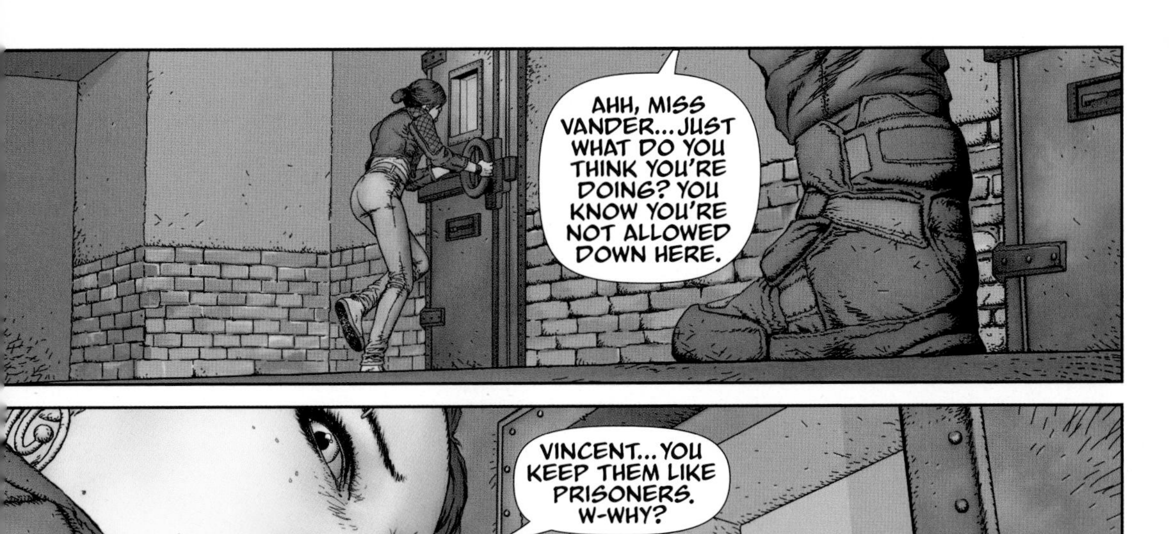
AHH, MISS VANDER...JUST WHAT DO YOU THINK YOU'RE DOING? YOU KNOW YOU'RE NOT ALLOWED DOWN HERE.
VINCENT...YOU KEEP THEM LIKE PRISONERS. W-WHY?

THEY ARE IN THE SAFEST PLACE THEY CAN BE. THERE'S SOMETHING YOU WILL COME TO LEARN.

Daily Note

MESSIAH_69

8/03/2048 23:12

I'm starting to believe that science and religion are the same thing, just from different perspectives. The Bible and other religious texts were left to help us understand but were widely misinterpreted, mistranslated (sometimes intentionally). God, man, the stars…it's all linked.

8/04/2048 02:41

What's more important: freedom or security? How free do people really want to be if they can't walk around without getting attacked? If they don't have food to eat? Freedom is an overrated luxury. And what's with all these idiots who want to interview me? Like I have time for that right now…

8/04/2048 22:49

The cube's visions have gotten REALLY dark since Dr. Vander joined in. She's got a dark past and a mind clouded with dark energy. I think I'm just using the word dark a lot because I'm tired. The will I've had to muster to finish this is unbelievable. They'll all thank me for it.

8/05/2048 00:34

Dr. Vander failed her test of loyalty. Vincent had to detain her overnight which is probably good since now we have the final carrier and it was an epigenetic change like I thought. NOTHING WILL STOP ME!

8/05/2048 06:15

We're out of time. It's today or we're shut down.

CHAPTER 3

ARE YOU TRYING TO RUIN EVERYTHING WE'VE BUILT? YOU KNOW MAINTAINING CONTACT WITH THE R-CARRIERS WAS PROTOCOL.

CONTACT, YES, NOT IMPRISON THEM. YOU'RE A F%$#KING MONSTER.
YOU THINK YOU'RE GOING TO GET AWAY WITH THIS?

THIS IS WRONG, SOME ARE CHILDREN. I SAW JESMINDER... SHE WAS TERRIFIED.
ARE ALL SIXTY-FOUR HERE?
NOAH HAD AN ARK. SO DO WE. YOU'RE ALL UNIQUE AND VITAL TO THE CUBE.

WHY NOT PAY THEM TO STAY? WHY WOULD YOU DO THIS?
BECAUSE IN THE FACE OF NECESSITY THERE IS NO ROOM FOR CHOICE.

NONE OF YOU RARE CARRIERS WERE BORN WITH THE DATA IN YOUR DNA.
IT'S AN EPIGENETIC CHANGE SOMETIME AFTER BIRTH. WE TESTED YOUR UMBILICAL CORD BLOOD THAT WAS BANKED...AND I TESTED THE OTHERS THAT I COULD.

IT'S WHY I HAD ETHAN TESTED AGAIN. HE IS POSITIVE NOW...HE HAS TO HAVE THE LAST PIECE.
WHAT?

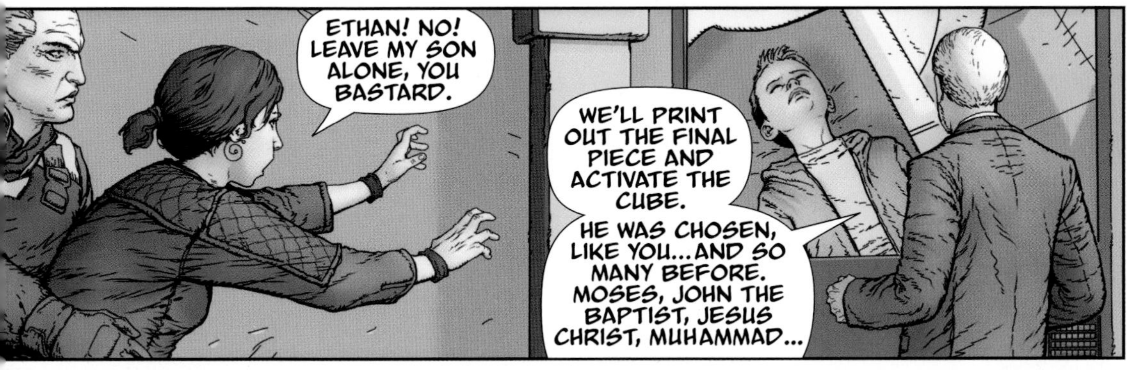
ETHAN! NO! LEAVE MY SON ALONE, YOU BASTARD.
WE'LL PRINT OUT THE FINAL PIECE AND ACTIVATE THE CUBE.
HE WAS CHOSEN, LIKE YOU...AND SO MANY BEFORE. MOSES, JOHN THE BAPTIST, JESUS CHRIST, MUHAMMAD...

THAT'S INSANE.
INSANITY IS MERELY AN ALTERNATE POINT OF VIEW.

PLEASE DON'T HURT MY SON.

HE'LL BE FINE. YOU HAVE MY WORD.
SUBJECT POSITIVE FOR EPIGENETIC CHANGES.

Six hundred and sixty-six pieces carried down through billions of people for millions of years.
And with that small step, it was finished.

The greatest puzzle in all of history was solved.
STAY BACK WHILE IT ASSIMILATES.

MMMMMMM

Has it been activated before? Perhaps, but we'll never know for sure.
MMMMMMMMMM

It would explain some weird historical anomalies.

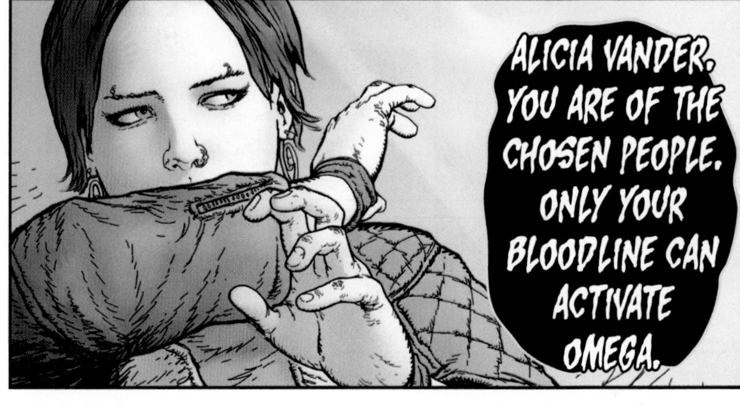
ALICIA VANDER, YOU ARE OF THE CHOSEN PEOPLE. ONLY YOUR BLOODLINE CAN ACTIVATE OMEGA.

YOU ARE REPRESENTATIVE OF YOUR KIND.

ARE YOU GOD?
I AM THAT I AM.

THE CHOICE IS YOURS.
WHAT CHOICE?

KRAKATHOOM
A SECOND CHANCE. YOUR TIME WILL REGRESS TWENTY-FIVE YEARS, BUT YOUR PEOPLE WILL RETAIN THE KNOWLEDGE OF THE PRESENT.
WHAT ABOUT MY SON?
HE WILL NO LONGER EXIST UNLESS YOU RECREATE HIM.

IS THAT A CERTAINTY?

IN AN EVER-CHANGING UNIVERSE, CERTAINTY IS IMPOSSIBLE.

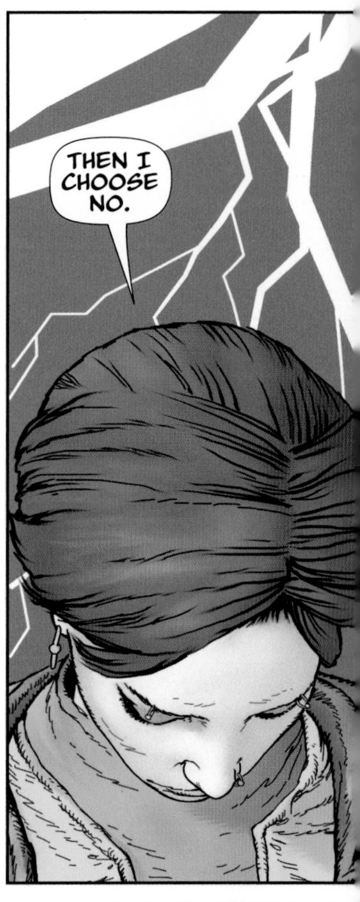
THEN I CHOOSE NO.

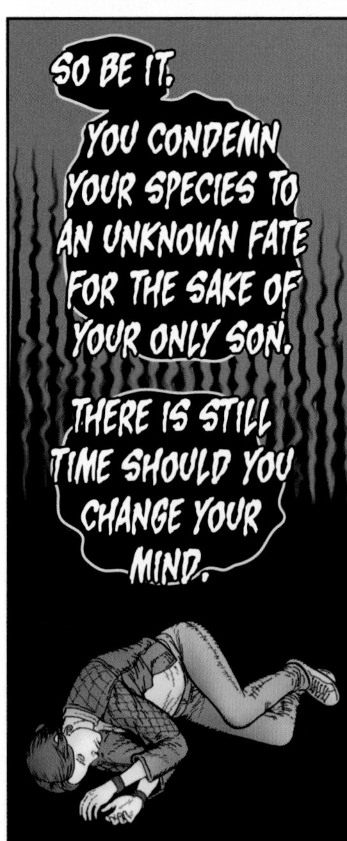
SO BE IT.
YOU CONDEMN YOUR SPECIES TO AN UNKNOWN FATE FOR THE SAKE OF YOUR ONLY SON.
THERE IS STILL TIME SHOULD YOU CHANGE YOUR MIND.

ETHAN.

YOU SON OF A BITCH. YOU KNEW, DIDN'T YOU? AND YOU DIDN'T CARE.

When I woke up, the cube, Alicia, Ethan, my control device...were gone.

ETHAN!

ARE YOU OKAY, BABY?
MOM? DID YOU SEE IT? THE CUBE? IT SPOKE TO ME.
YES, I SAW IT TOO, WE CAN TALK ABOUT THAT LATER. WE NEED TO GET OUT OF HERE.

08/05/2048
10:28
I CALLED YOUR DAD AND HE'S GOING TO MEET US. I DON'T KNOW WHO ELSE WE CAN TRUST RIGHT NOW.
MOM, THE CUBE... IT'S A GOOD THING. IT GIVES US A SECOND CHANCE. A BETTER LIFE. WE CAN LEARN FROM OUR MISTAKES.

THAT SECOND CHANCE COULD WIPE OUT YOUR EXISTENCE, IT'S NOT A RISK I'M WILLING TO TAKE.

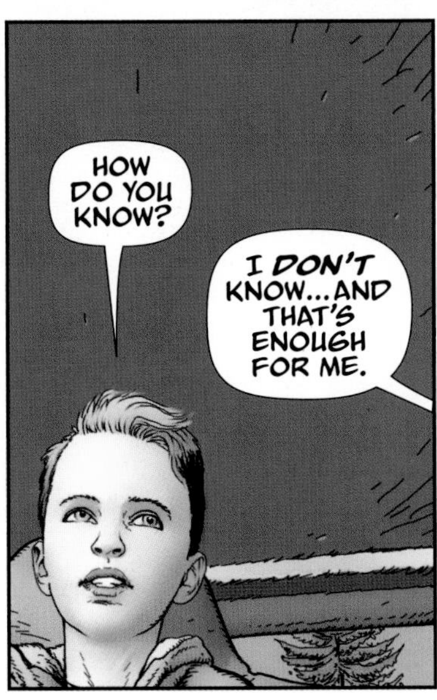
HOW DO YOU KNOW?
I DON'T KNOW...AND THAT'S ENOUGH FOR ME.

THERE'S YOUR DAD.

GET IN.
LEAVE MY CAR HERE?
WE'LL GET IT LATER... PLEASE, NICK.

WHAT IS GOING ON?
I NEED TO GO PUBLIC AND STOP HOPKINS FROM ACTIVATING THE CUBE.

THE CUBE ISN'T WHAT HE'S BEEN CLAIMING. IT'S SOME SORT OF TEMPORAL DEVICE THAT SETS OUR TIMELINE BACK TWENTY-FIVE YEARS. IT'LL CHANGE US BY DESTROYING US.

THAT'S NUTTY.
IT'S TRUE, DAD, THE CUBE SPOKE TO ME TOO.
IT'S NOT GOD. I DON'T THINK IT'S EVEN RELIGIOUS. IT'S SOME SORT OF ARTIFICIAL INTELLIGENCE.

THAT'S KIND OF HARD TO BELIEVE.
MORE THAN A MAN BORN OF A VIRGIN MOTHER WHO'S BOTH GOD AND HIS SON...DIED AND WAS RESURRECTED?
POINT.

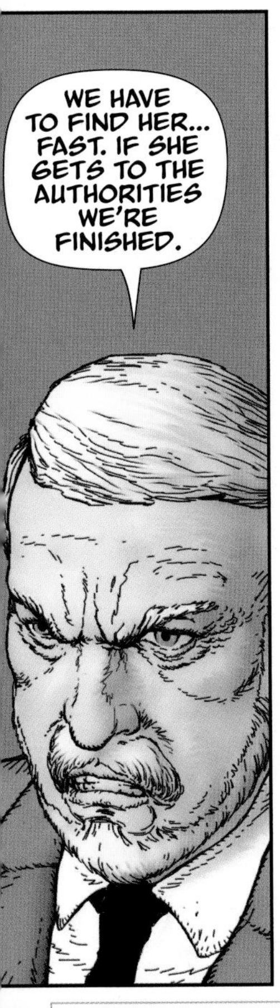
WE HAVE TO FIND HER... FAST. IF SHE GETS TO THE AUTHORITIES WE'RE FINISHED.

WE'VE GOT TRACKERS ON BOTH DR. VANDER AND THE BOY. THEY WON'T GET FAR.

I genuinely regret the sequence of events that followed, the people that were killed, but I really didn't know what else to do. There was no time for hesitation.

I knew by setting the timeline back, anyone who died in the intervening time would return to life.

So who exactly have I murdered?
Should a man be held accountable for a crime in an alternate dimension when the end result saved all of humanity?

08/05/2048
12:41
IF YOU'RE THE ONLY ONE WHO CAN ACTIVATE IT...WHY DO ANYTHING?

I DON'T KNOW THAT I'M THE ONLY ONE. ANY OF THE RARE CARRIERS MIGHT BE ABLE TO.

IT SPOKE OF SOME BLOODLINE, I DON'T KNOW. WE JUST CAN'T TAKE THE CHANCE. I'M REALLY SCARED, NICK.
WE'VE GOT COMPANY.

TARGET PAINTED, UPLOADING COORDINATES.

TAKE THE WOMAN AND CHILD ALIVE, NO FORCE RESTRICTIONS.
ROGER THAT.
TAXI

TAKE OUT A CAR IN FRONT OF THEM.

ONE ROADBLOCK COMING UP.

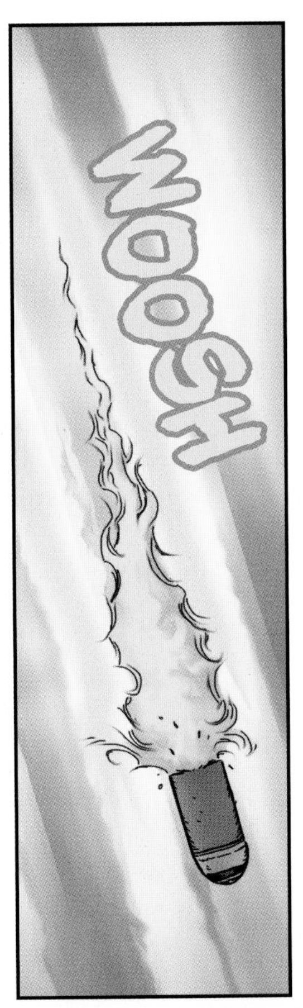
WOOSH

BOOM

THERE'S A STATE TROOPER RIGHT THERE.

RRRRTT

HEY! THOSE PEOPLE ARE TRYING TO KILL US.

THEY HAVE MILITARY TRANSPONDERS.
CALL IT IN ANYWAY.
POLICE

THIS IS A GOVERNMENT OPERATION, THAT WOMAN IS A KNOWN TERRORIST.
TAKE THEM OUT.

SHE'S NOT GOING ANYWHERE... WE JUST CALLED IT IN, GIVE US A--

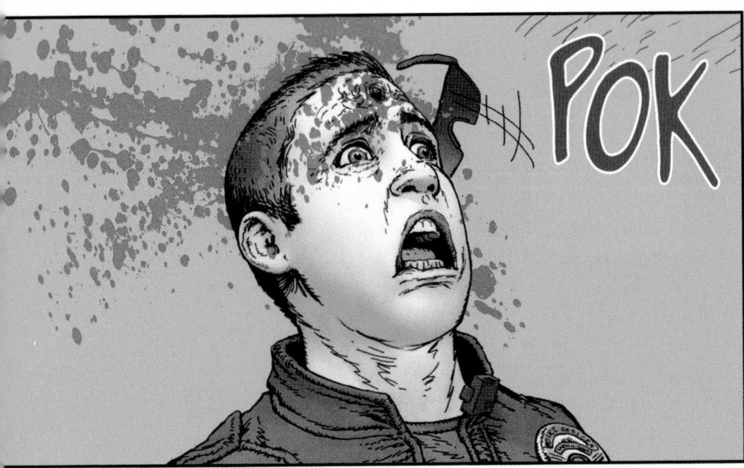
POK

GRAB THEM.

OFFICER DOWN, MULTIPLE ARMED COMBATANTS, NEED BACKUP IMMEDIATELY.

WHAT ARE YOU WAITING FOR?
I...UH... USED TO BE A COP.

POK

I've since spoken to both those officers and arranged a settlement with them.
WHY ARE THEY TRYING TO KILL US?
IF THEY WANTED US DEAD WE'D BE DEAD ALREADY.
THEY WANT THE CUBE ACTIVATED. HE THINKS HE CAN DO IT WITH THAT DEVICE HE MADE, BUT I'M NOT SURE IF THAT WILL WORK.

THEY'RE GAINING ON US.

ELIMINATE THE MALE.

THEY KILLED COPS, HELP IS ON THE WAY. WE JUST HAVE TO--

POK

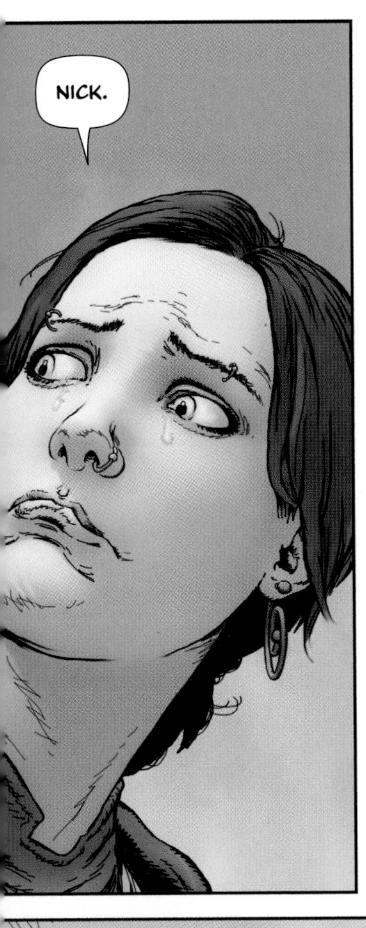
NICK.

DID SOMETHING HAPPEN TO DAD?
NO...HE'S LEADING THEM AWAY FROM US. JUST RUN, HONEY.

My one major miscalculation was love.
I underestimated how much Dr. Vander loved her son. I thought her autism would prevent a deep emotional bond between mother and child.

WILL THESE PEOPLE GET HURT?

I DON'T KNOW, HONEY. WE NEED TO FIND SOMEWHERE TO HIDE UNTIL THE POLICE GET HERE.

WE'VE LOST CONTROL. POLICE AND MILITARY SCRAMBLING TO INTERCEPT US NOW.
WE'VE GOT LESS THAN SIX MINUTES TO ACTIVATE BEFORE WE'RE SWARMED.

ROGER THAT. FIRST RESPONDERS ALMOST CONTAINED.

POLICE
EXFIL STRATEGY?
NONE. WE ACTIVATE HERE AND NOW OR WE'RE ALL DEAD.
POLICE

KILL THEM ALL, VANDER AND HER SON, TOO. JUST GET THE DEVICE.

CLOSED
DAD'S DEAD, ISN'T HE?
NO, HONEY.

VINCENT... PLEASE DON'T HURT ETHAN.

WE'RE WELL PAST THAT, DOCTOR.

KRAK

WHUMP

MOM... MOMMY... ARE YOU OKAY?

MOMMY?

WE'VE GOT MASSIVE INCOMING, TWO MINUTES.

ETHAN, THE CHOICE IS YOURS.
WHAT WILL HAPPEN?
A SECOND CHANCE FOR THIS WORLD.
WILL MOMMY AND DADDY BE ALIVE?

YES.
DO I PRESS THIS BUTTON?
IF THAT IS HOW YOU CHOOSE YES, THE CHOICE IS YOURS.

ETHAN, GIVE ME THE DEVICE.

YES.

What happened next is public record.

AHHH!

I think we all remember.

It was glorious.
AS IT IS WRITTEN.

SO SHALL IT BE DONE.

42

The world was remade.

I don't know how, but I knew in that moment...

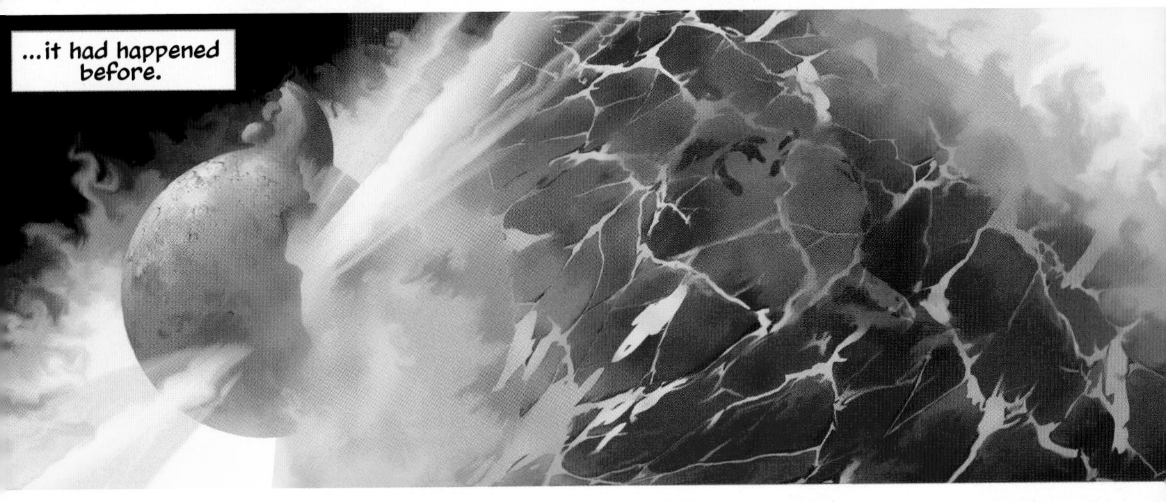
...it had happened before.

Glory, glory, hallelujah.

Oblivion claimed us. We were all aware... all one...but without body or form.

Humanity had its
second birth.

WASHINGTON, DC
9/13/2023
AND THAT'S HOW WE ENDED UP HERE. WE AND THE WORLD ARE ALL TWENTY-FIVE YEARS YOUNGER WITH MEMORIES OF EVERYTHING THAT HAPPENED.
INDIA AND PAKISTAN HAVE BOTH STARTED DISMANTLING THEIR NUCLEAR ARSENALS.
THE ENVIRONMENTAL EFFORTS TO CURTAIL WHAT WE SAW HAVE BEEN EMBRACED WORLDWIDE. THERE ARE NO MORE DENIERS, THE DEBATE IS OVER.
FORTY-THREE PERCENT OF THE WORLD POPULATION IS NOW GONE.
MY OWN SON WAS IN THAT GROUP. MY EX-WIFE AND I HAVE RECONCILED AND WANT TO TRY AND RECREATE HIM.

THERE'S ALSO THE TWO PLUS BILLION THAT HAVE RETURNED FROM THE DEAD.
WE'VE SEEN THE REAL CONSEQUENCES OF OUR ACTIONS. WE HAVE A REAL SECOND CHANCE TO MAKE THE WORLD A BETTER PLACE FOR EVERYONE, NOT JUST THE WEALTHY.
IF I'M TO BE THROWN IN A CELL TO LIVE OUT MY DAYS, I GO WILLINGLY KNOWING I SACRIFICED EVERYTHING FOR THE GREATER GOOD.

YOU WON'T BE HELD, YOU'RE FREE TO GO.

THEY LET YOU JUST WALK RIGHT OUT OF THERE?
I SAVED THE WORLD.

DID YOU TELL THEM DR. VANDER AND THE OTHER RARE CARRIERS WERE NO LONGER HUMAN?

I DID NOT. WE NEED TO HAVE SOME ADVANTAGE GOING FORWARD, DON'T WE?

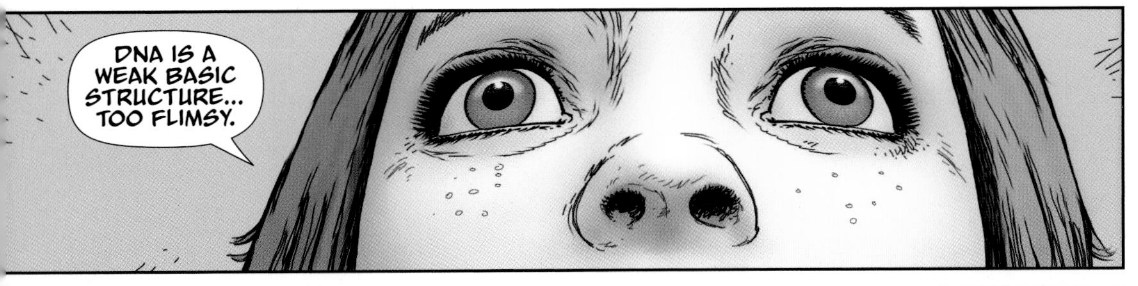
DNA IS A WEAK BASIC STRUCTURE... TOO FLIMSY.

THIS IS BETTER.

HUMANS ARE MAINLY CARBON-12, A MOLECULE WITH SIX PROTONS, SIX NEUTRONS AND SIX ELECTRONS.
THE MORNING STAR IS PHOSPHORUS.

COMBINING PHOSPHORUS WITH CARBON-12 CREATES A FORM OF HUMAN DNA.
HOPKINS IS BEING HAILED A HERO FOR ACTIVATING THE DEVICE.

HERO MY ASS...MY SON ACTIVATED THE DEVICE.
THE END?

Daily Note

MESSIAH_69

8/06/2048 09:24

This is my first journal entry after the event. The event, the device…is this from an artificial intelligence like Dr. Vander believes? Or is it God? I used to make fun of religious people, but after all that I don't even know what to think anymore. Temporal science or miracle? So much to do, wow I feel so much better and stronger now. Twenty-five years makes a big difference. It's nice to feel young again!

8/07/2032 10:32

The dead that have been rolled back have no memory after their death. That makes sense I suppose, sucks for those that died of old age twenty-five years ago today. Can you imagine coming back for one day then dying again? Well fortunately for most the picture is rosier.

8/09/2023 14:04

My ex-wife and I have reconciled. I want to have children, but no Peters. Won't make that mistake again.

8/11/2023 00:34

Lawyers tell me I'm about to be arrested and detained. I knew that was coming. They'll figure it out. I saved the world, they should worship me.

SCIENCE CLASS

Welcome to STAIRWAY! For you Kickstarter backers, thank you again for your patience with this one. Life intervenes at times, but I hope you're happy with this final read. If you want to click these links, but don't want to type them in, you can go to my blog site **http://matttalks.com/** and I'll have posted the links there along with this science class and you can click through from there.

STORING DATA IN DNA

This is real. Harvard geneticists George Church, Sri Kosuri and colleagues have been storing digital data in DNA since 2012. They "encoded a 52,000-word book in thousands of snippets of DNA, using strands of DNA's four-letter alphabet of A, G, T, and C to encode the 0s and 1s of the digitized file." DNA storage could solve a lot of problems. According to some stats I've seen (they conflict) we've amassed 90% of the world's data in the last decade and it's doubling every few years. I can't find accurate numbers, seems no one knows for sure. We could store ALL of the world's current data in a single small room using DNA to store it. DNA regenerates and is passed down from generation to generation, so it is a viable possibility to store data for billions of years. Once I made that leap in my mind, STAIRWAY kind of flowed. If it is possible to store data on DNA and we used to call the DNA we didn't know what it did junk DNA, then it's possible someone left information there from a long, long time ago. Some of the earlier drafts of this story had WAY more in-depth science of all this, but I eventually stripped it out and left most of it for here. Lots of links, central to the story and all plausible, so please check some of these out!

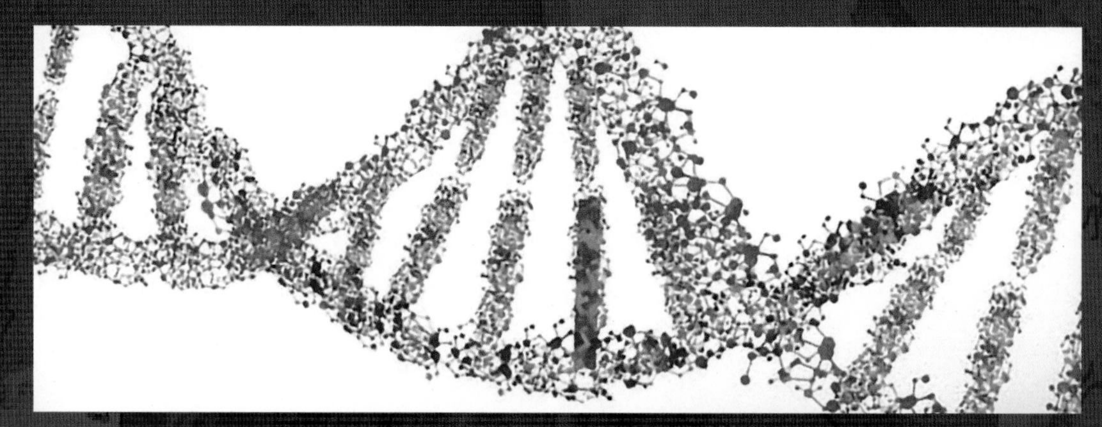

"According to computer giant IBM, 2.5 exabytes - that's 2.5 billion gigabytes (GB) - of data was generated every day in 2012."

» **http://www.bbc.com/news/business-26383058**

"A bioengineer and geneticist at Harvard's Wyss Institute have successfully stored 5.5 petabits of data — around 700 terabytes — in a single gram of DNA, smashing the previous DNA data density record by a thousand times."

» **http://www.sciencemag.org/news/2017/03/dna-could-store-all-worlds-data-one-room**

» **https://www.extremetech.com/extreme/134672-harvard-cracks-dna-storage-crams-700-terabytes-of-data-into-a-single-gram**

» **https://www.zdnet.com/article/microsofts-dna-storage-breakthrough-could-pave-way-for-exabyte-drives/**

Running out of data storage space?

» **https://blog.seagate.com/intelligent/world-run-data-storage-capacity/**

» **https://www.statista.com/statistics/751749/worldwide-data-storage-capacity-and-demand/**

THE HISTORY OF DNA

1859

Charles Darwin's *On the Origin of Species* introduces the theory of evolution, the idea that inherited characteristics change over generations. Initially the idea was discussed only in regard to plants and animals, because many religious people considered the notion that humans evolved from other animals to be blasphemous.

The question of whether modern life forms could have descended from more primitive creatures is very old. The ancient Greeks and Chinese debated the idea more than two thousand years ago.

1866

Gregor Mendel discovers the basis of genetics, the principle that traits are inherited by offspring in discrete units that today we call "genes." The significance of Mendel's work was not recognized by scientists until decades later.

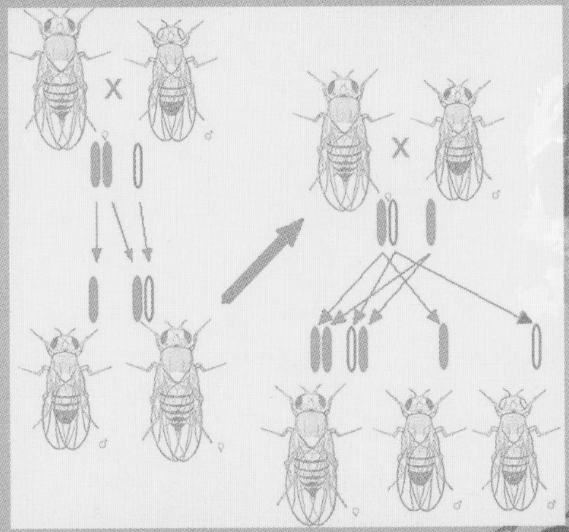

1869

Friedrich Miescher identifies nucleic acids, essential bio-molecules found in all living things. Nucleic acids encode the information that directs the functioning of each living cell.

1900s

In the late 1800s, Francis Galton coins the term eugenics ("well-born") for a belief that the quality of human traits can be improved through selective breeding and the sterilization of "undesirables." Eugenics was practiced in the United States and Germany prior to World War II.

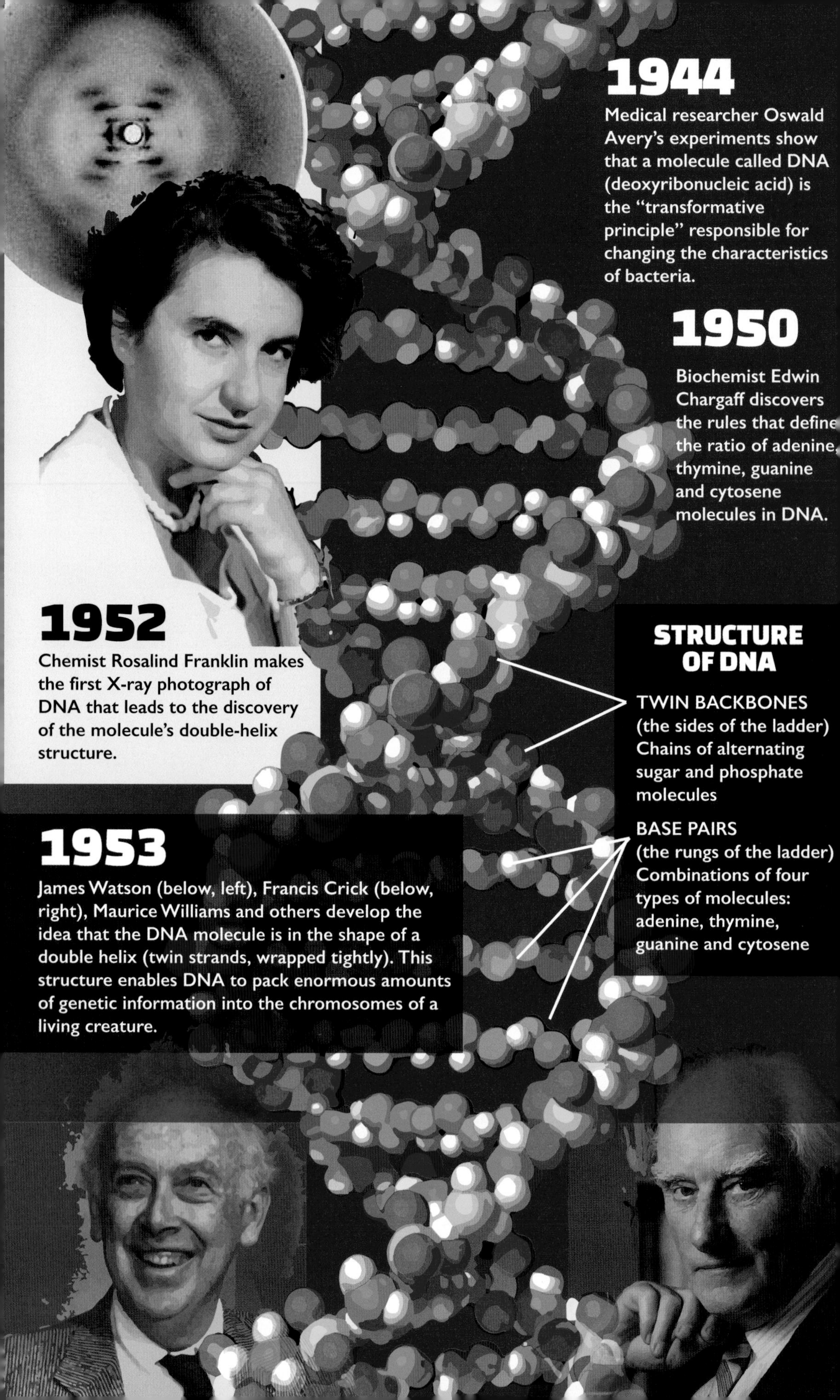
1944
Medical researcher Oswald Avery's experiments show that a molecule called DNA (deoxyribonucleic acid) is the "transformative principle" responsible for changing the characteristics of bacteria.
1950
Biochemist Edwin Chargaff discovers the rules that define the ratio of adenine, thymine, guanine and cytosene molecules in DNA.
1952
Chemist Rosalind Franklin makes the first X-ray photograph of DNA that leads to the discovery of the molecule's double-helix structure.
STRUCTURE OF DNA
TWIN BACKBONES (the sides of the ladder) Chains of alternating sugar and phosphate molecules
BASE PAIRS (the rungs of the ladder) Combinations of four types of molecules: adenine, thymine, guanine and cytosene
1953
James Watson (below, left), Francis Crick (below, right), Maurice Williams and others develop the idea that the DNA molecule is in the shape of a double helix (twin strands, wrapped tightly). This structure enables DNA to pack enormous amounts of genetic information into the chromosomes of a living creature.

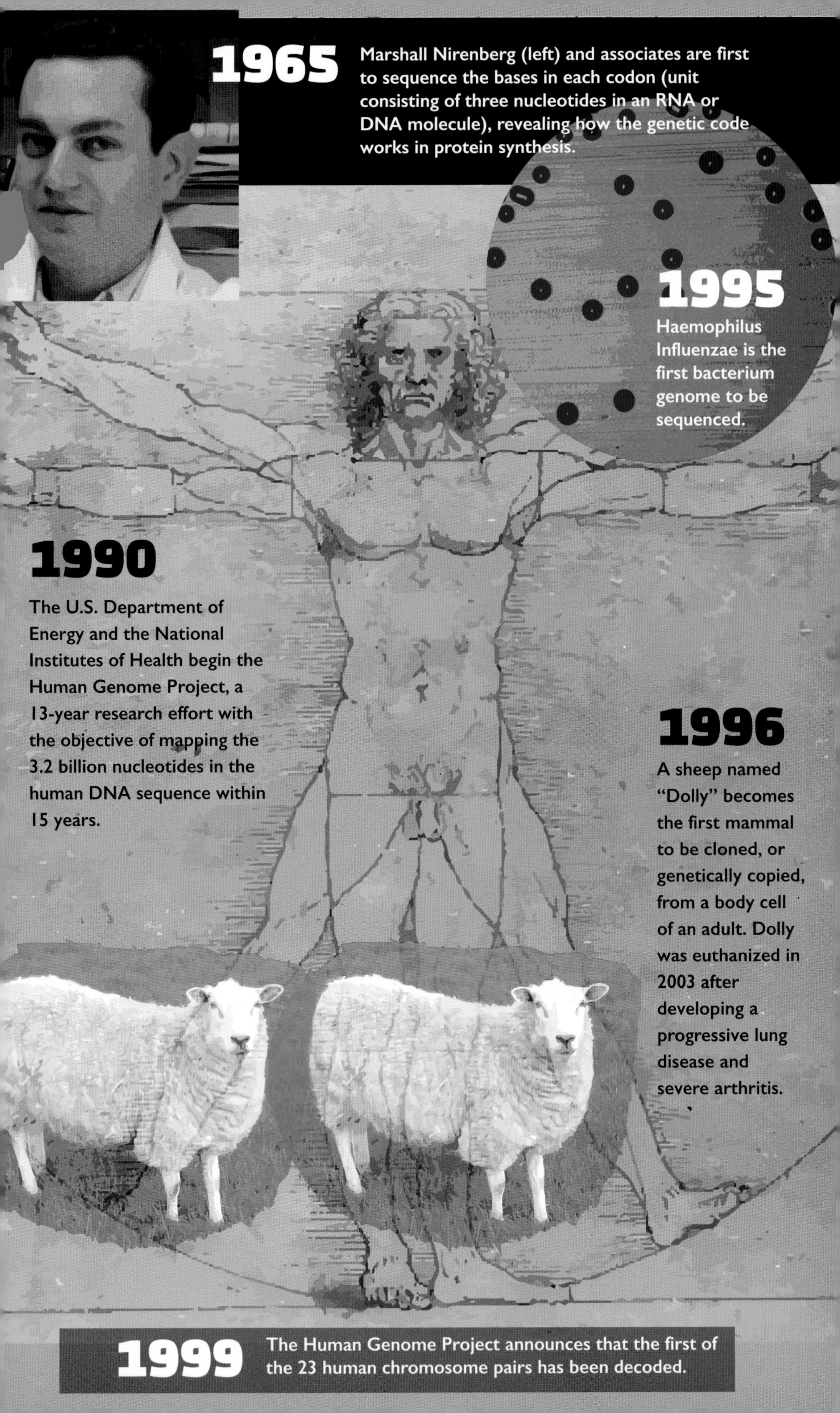

1965
Marshall Nirenberg (left) and associates are first to sequence the bases in each codon (unit consisting of three nucleotides in an RNA or DNA molecule), revealing how the genetic code works in protein synthesis.
1995
Haemophilus Influenzae is the first bacterium genome to be sequenced.
1990
The U.S. Department of Energy and the National Institutes of Health begin the Human Genome Project, a 13-year research effort with the objective of mapping the 3.2 billion nucleotides in the human DNA sequence within 15 years.
1996
A sheep named "Dolly" becomes the first mammal to be cloned, or genetically copied, from a body cell of an adult. Dolly was euthanized in 2003 after developing a progressive lung disease and severe arthritis.
1999
The Human Genome Project announces that the first of the 23 human chromosome pairs has been decoded.

2000

The fruit fly genome is decoded.

2002

The genome of a mouse is decoded. For the first time, scientists can compare the human genome with another mammal.

2003

The Human Genome Project is completed.

2012

Harvard scientists discover that DNA can be "written to" like data on a computer's hard drive by using CRISPR, a powerful genetic editing tool first used in the 1980s. CRISPR stands for "Clustered Regularly Interspaced Short Palindromic Repeats."

2014

Scientists create an organism with an expanded genome by adding artificial nucleotides, or extra "letters," to its DNA code.

2018

Modifications to the CRISPR genome editing technique make it more versatile.

INFOGRAPHIC BY KARL TATE. SOURCES: DNAWORLDWIDE.COM, WIKIPEDIA, U.S. NATIONAL INSTITUTES OF HEALTH, NATIONAL CANCER INSTITUTE

http://blog.newspapers.library.in.gov/the-black-stork-eugenics-goes-to-the-movies/

https://www.cancer.gov/about-nci/organization/ccg/blog/2015/CRISPRa

NDIAN/PAKISTANI NUCLEAR WAR

was initially going to go with India and China nuking each other, but I've always found this conflict more interesting. If China and India go to war, it's likely to be about water and has been going on for a long, long time. The Indian/Pakistani issue is either old or new depending on how you look at it. Both countries were part of the colonial British Empire and are struggling to deal with modern borders and ancient rivalries. After WWII the British partitioned India into roughly its modern layout and India/Pakistan have had three wars since then. They're both nuclear states, they border each other and there are tribal and religious ifferences that cause drama. I'm no expert on this conflict, but I found it interesting enough to base that conflict as an inciting incident. Read more at the links below:

- **https://www.economist.com/news/special-report/21725099-three-score-and-ten-years-after-their-acrimonious-split-india-and-pakistan-remain**
- **http://foreignpolicy.com/2014/02/04/why-india-and-pakistan-hate-each-other/**

CUBE CONSTRUCTION

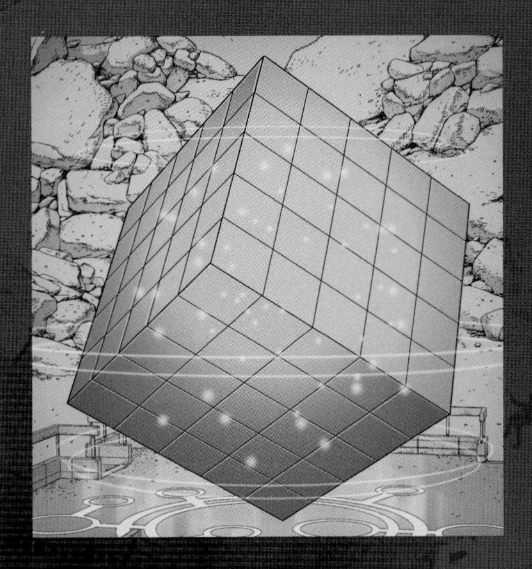

left this somewhat unclear in the story on purpose, but the C and R carrier construction through the DNA is only one method of this sentience/artificial intelligence manifesting. Lots of hints at previous mysteries, arcana, paranormal, prophesies, etc. There's so much fun you could have telling stories with this thing throughout time. In my study of history there are always important leaps of technology or innovation that seem to change everything for a period of time. What if this cube's time reset is the explanation for some of those?

TWENTY-FIVE YEAR TIME RESET

Raffaele Ienco actually came up with the idea f the time reset when we were talking about his initially. I was planning something a bit darker and more end-times oriented rather than a straight up rebirth scenario. I had the idea for the DNA discovery, the cube, etc., but in those initial talks I didn't know what it would actually do. When he suggested that I started thinking about it and the story flowed from there. Most time travel stories are about an individual or two, so warping out the whole population seemed kind of fun and different and opened up a lot of other story possibilities. Does the time reset just affect earth or is it the whole universe? Some interesting other possibilities to play with in that line of thinking as well.

also liked the idea a bit that this kind of doesn't make sense when you really think about it. Who made the Cube? Why would they do it this way? Why 25 years? Why not 100 years? Are the cube creators still alive? If not and it's a rogue A.I. what was it's real original function? The ways you can go with a story like this is part of the fun of it.

GREGORY HOPKINS

There were so many narrative Hopkins captions that I wrote, deleted, rewrote, etc. When I first wrote this book it was with Alicia Vander narratives. After one draft that way it didn't work and I thought about switching to Hopkins. Is he the bad guy? Is he a utilitarian pragmatist? s he the savior of the world? To me he can be all three of those things. I wrote him pre-event as feeling victimized. After the event he's still an asshole, but he's been changed somewhat and even might have some belief in something bigger than himself. I really can't stand one-note villains. Every villain is the hero of their own story. This live science link is worth reading, talks about how people like this victimize themselves and justify heinous shit.

- **https://www.livescience.com/51476-how-amoral-people-justify-their-crimes.html**

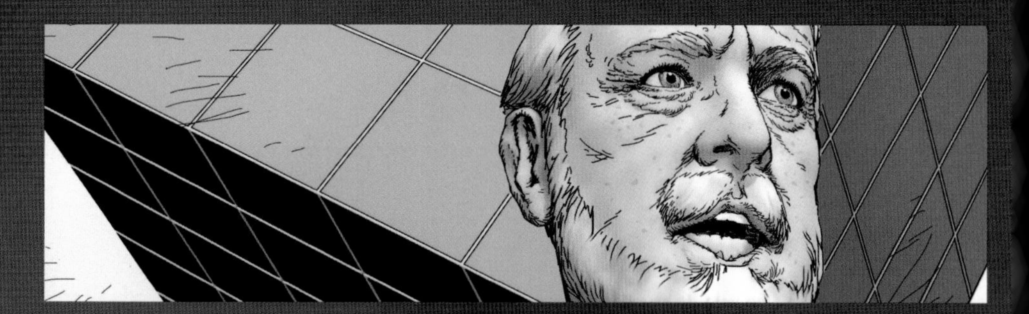

SOME DELETED HOPKINS CAPS I LIKED:

Gregory Cap: Do the means justify the ends? I don't know...but I saved the world and th has to mean something.

Gregory Cap: It affected my mind. I was so obsessed with it. I can only explain my interactic with it as a religious experience.

Gregory Cap: A certain euphoria.

Gregory Cap: "The mass of men lead lives of quiet desperation." —Always enjoye Thoreau's quote it's too bad he was such a granola-head pussy.

Gregory Cap: Only great men can do what needs to be done...I'm going to save the wor So what if a few billion people have to die.

Gregory Cap: The needs of the many do outweigh the needs of the few, so killing some them should be ok.

Gregory Cap: Is it murder when a child drowns in the ocean because he's not strong enoug to swim against the current? Or is it the natural selection of our species to reproduc stronger organisms?

666 THE NUMBER OF THE BEAST

My two great fascinations in life are religion and science. I love them both. I was raised Baptist and have studied the Bible and almost all religious texts thoroughly. I'm an athei but I'm not anti-religion and I'm fine with what you believe as long as you don't want to k me or force me to do anything I don't want to do. So what does 666 actually mean? Fro the second link below: "According to the last book in the Bible, 666 is the number, or nam of the wild beast with seven heads and ten horns that comes out of the sea. (Revelatic 13:1, 17, 18) This beast is a symbol of the worldwide political system, which rules over 'eve tribe and people and tongue and nation.'" (Revelation 13:7) The name 666 identifies th political system as a gross failure in God's sight." According to the third link below it was secret code at the time which stood for Nero Caesar. "When you actually look at the origin text, you'll see that in this passage, the letters of 666 are actually written in Hebrew, whic places a higher significance on numbers meaning words and words meaning numbers tha ancient Greek. The writer was very clearly trying to tell us something.

"And sure enough, if you translate the Hebrew spelling of 666, you actually spell out Nerc Kesar - the Hebrew spelling of Nero Caesar."

We've all heard the stories of the antichrist and the "Beast" from Revelations and the have been SO MANY times people have proclaimed we're in that end time. I've heard it least six times in my own lifetime and I'm not even at the half century mark...just yet.

- **https://www.huffingtonpost.com/2013/01/22/common-misconception abo_n_2489899.html**
- **https://www.jw.org/en/bible-teachings/questions/what-does-666-mean/**
- **https://www.sciencealert.com/what-is-the-secret-meaning-behind-the-devil-number-666-mathematics**
- **https://gnosticwarrior.com/science-of-666.html**

MEANING OF APOCALYPSE

The literal, original meaning of apocalypse is an uncovering, a revealing or an unveiling. It was predominantly used about secret truths. Christianity was not well received initially and took a long time to take over. Early Christians were persecuted for their beliefs so they would convey things in code. If you look at the 666 comment above, what's more likely, that the people at the time were talking in code about the political system at the time? Or that they were laying out a massive series of prophecies for the end times that were so vague that just about every generation has thought they were in that end time prophesied?

CUBE IN GOLGOTHA AND THIS CUBE

They're linked, yes. GOLGOTHA V2 will be out in mid-2019, STAIRWAY V2 by end of 2019. Interesting that cubes have been used in religions, the Muslims pray to one 5 times a day.

» **http://www.ancient-origins.net/artifacts-other-artifacts/kaaba-black-stone-holy-stone-outer-space-003661**

RELIGIOUS SYMBOLISM AND ENOCHIAN LANGUAGE

There are so many religious symbols, the one most familiar to us in the west is the cross. They all have power that we give them through our belief and use. Art, history, government...all of these things are intertwined with religion and its symbolism. The Book of Enoch is an old Jewish text that is not accepted by all Jewish scholars. There are a lot of books that could have been included in the Bible including the gnostic gospels of the New Testament. I encourage you to read them, they're fascinating. Even if just to arm yourself with why they weren't included (if you're a believer).

DOWNLOAD THE BOOK OF ENOCH FREE HERE:
» **http://scriptural-truth.com/images/BookOfEnoch.pdf**

GOOD OVERALL SYMBOL DISCUSSION:
» **https://www.britannica.com/topic/religious-symbolism**
» **https://www.ancient-symbols.com/religious_symbols.html**

DOWNLOAD THE BOOK OF ENOCH FREE HERE:
» **http://scriptural-truth.com/images/BookOfEnoch.pdf**

GOOD OVERALL SYMBOL DISCUSSION:
» **https://www.britannica.com/topic/religious-symbolism**
» **https://www.ancient-symbols.com/religious_symbols.html**

NUCLEAR WAR ENVIRONMENTAL EFFECTS

So as a child of the Cold War and a student of physics, I've been stressed about nuclear war my entire life. I read about the Manhattan Projects and some of the early physicists' fear that the testing might set the atmosphere on fire. Meaning we set off a few nukes and it kills the entire planet. This didn't happen, but the fear still remains. The long term environmental effects of a nuclear war, even a limited one like I've outlined in this story, would be devastating. There's no question we'd have a worldwide economic collapse, disruption of shipping and severe environment damage. There's so much of this online I'm just going to link it, do a deep dive you'll get lost in it, I promise!

CASTLE BRAVO TESTING:

» **https://www.youtube.com/watch?v=uFY5k_3BInk**

SET ATMOSPHERE ON FIRE:

» **https://blogs.scientificamerican.com/cross-check/bethe-teller-trinity-and-the-end-of-earth/**

DEBUNKED:

» **https://www.metabunk.org/debunked-scientists-risked-destroying-the-earth-during-nuclear-tests-and-cern.t692/**

ENVIRONMENTAL EFFECTS OF NUCLEAR WAR:

» **https://www.quora.com/How-many-nukes-would-it-take-to-cause-a-minor-nuclear-winter-What-about-a-moderate-one**
» **https://daily.jstor.org/the-environmental-impact-of-nuclear-war/**
» **http://theconversation.com/even-a-minor-nuclear-war-would-be-an-ecological-disaster-felt-throughout-the-world-82288**
» **https://physicstoday.scitation.org/doi/full/10.1063/1.3047679**

SCIENCE FICTION/RELIGIOUS THEMES

Atheists 50 years ago felt there would be a mass movement away from religious belief once humanity became more technologically advanced. Science would replace religion was the thought. Well...that hasn't happened really at all. Church attendance is down in the USA, but belief seems to be the same. If anything, we have more extremists now than ever before. Social media and the internet allow a bunch of yahoos to find their yahoo buddies and go be extreme together.

PETAHERTZ COMMUNICATION

This was a bit of a stab in the dark on what sort of tech we'd have in this near-term future. I think we're more likely to be sending data on light waves by then, but this was an easy way to do it. Right now we are about to start communicating in 5G which according to Wikipedia is, "The primary technologies include: Millimeter wave bands (26, 28, 38, and 60 GHz) offering performance as high as 20 gigabits per second (Gbit/s); Massive MIMO (Multiple Input Multiple Output - 64-256 antennas) offering performance 'up to ten times current 4G networks;' 'Low-band 5G' and 'Mid-band 5G' using frequencies from 600 MHz to 6 GHz, especially 3.5-4.2 GHz."

» **Millimeter wavelength communication**
» **http://ethw.org/Millimeter_Waves**
» **https://ieeexplore.ieee.org/abstract/document/55923/?reload=true**
» **https://www.sciencedaily.com/releases/2018/02/180206115340.htm**

GENERATIONAL POPULATION

If you use a 25.5 year mean generation length, everyone is related to everyone from about 4,000 years ago. It makes genetic research interesting.

» **http://articles.latimes.com/2013/may/07/science/la-sci-european-dna-20130508**

That's it for now! STAIRWAY V2 will hit sometime in late 2019. Thanks for reading, and if you like this book, please recommend it to a friend and give us a review on Amazon and Good Reads!

Carpe Diem,

Matt Hawkins
Twitter: @topcowmatt
Facebook.com/selfloathingnarcissist

MATT HAWKINS

A veteran of the initial Image Comics launch, Matt started his career in comic book publishing in 1993 and has been working with Image as a creator, writer and executive for over 25 years. President/COO of Top Cow since 1998, Matt has created and written over 30 new franchises for Top Cow and Image including THINK TANK, THE TITHE: SAMARITAN, POSTAL, GOLGOTHA, WARFRAME, APHRODITE IX and SWING as well as handling the company's business affairs.

OTHER TITLES FROM MATT THAT YOU MAY ENJOY:

THINK TANK VOL. 1 (978-1607066606)
THE TITHE VOL. 1 (978-1632153241)
GOLGOTHA (978-1534303201)

RAFFAELE "RAFF" IENCO

A comic book creator who has been in the industry for more than twenty years, and whose works have been published most recently by both Marvel and Image Comics. Raff's creator-owned works include the EPIC KILL series and the graphic novels DEVOID OF LIFE *and* MANIFESTATIONS. His work for Top Cow includes SYMMETRY, MECHANISM, and POSTAL. He has also worked for DC Comics on *Batman: Sins of the Father*. Born in Italy, he came to Canada when he was 4 and currently lives in Toronto.

OTHER TITLES FROM RAFFAELE THAT YOU MAY ENJOY:

EPIC KILL VOL. 1 (978-1607066286)
MECHANISM (978-1534300323)
SYMMETRY (978-1632156990)

KICKSTARTER THANK YOU!

Aaron Scholz
Aaron Sorensen
Abel Cervantes
AceArtemis7
Adam Finer
Adam Quantrill
Adam Taylor
Alan Smith
Alina Schimpf
Amrit Birdi
Amy Quinn
Andrew John
Anthony Rivera
Anthony Spay
Antonio A Rodriguez
Antonio Campos Jr
Art DeWitt
Austin Allen Hamblin
Avatar
Ben Lalonde
Ben Rosenthal
Benjamin Alexander
Benoit Pierre
Blarghedy
Bob Axell
Bobbi Boyd
Brad Bailey
Bradley Bradley
Brian Anderson
Brian Beardsley
Brian Berling
Brian Bolvin
Brian Flinn
Brian Laliberte
Britt Eubanks
bryan pickering
Bryce Undy
CA Preece
carlos giffoni
Carlos Giffoni
Chad Nuss
Charles Cornwall
Charon Comics
Chris Johnson
Chris Skuller
Chris Wyatt
Christina Gale
Christopher “Kier” Conroy
Christopher Preece
CHUC Fabien
Claude
Craig Rodenhauser
Craig Soffer
Crayton Matthews
Cris Ann Clay
Curtis Herink
D Kelly
D Michael Martinez
D van Rappard
Dale Wilson
Dan
Dan Gibson
Dan Rivera
Daniel Chng
Daniel Lin
Daniel Theodore
Danielle Michelucci
David Armour
David Geye
David Kastner
David Malyn
David Mayo
David Penner
David Phan
David Yu Chen
Deirdre Benson
Derek
Derek J. Bush
Devin Cannon
DeZinna
Dom G
Donald Stewart
Douggie Sharpe
Dwayne Farver
Dylan Andrews
Daniel ‘Woody” Weber
Eddie James Carswell II
Eddy Moreno
Eileen M.
Ellen Power
Elliot Blake
Emily Peacock
ENRIQUE F LOPEZ
(STUDIO MA-EN)
Erasmus Fox, Inc.
Eric Palicki
Ernesto
Ethan Belanger
Eugene Alejandro
Eva Jarkiewicz
Felipe Cagno
Fermin Serena Hortas
Frank Martin
Fredrik Holmqvist
Gavin Andazola
Giancarlo Caracuzzo
GMark C
Greene County Creative
Gregory Shane Helms
Gretchen Anthony
Guest 330781646
Guest 635686725
Gwen.
Haevermaet Anthony
Harpreet Miglani
Hereticked
HOK
Ian Yarington
Iran Romaldo
Jackson
Jacob Bear
Jake Combs
James Azrael
James Ferguson
James R. Crowley
Jaroslaw Ejsymont
Jason Beltram
Jason Crase
Jason LeConey
Jay Lofstead
Jeff Karl
Jen
Jeremiah Bell
jesse
Jesse Golden-Marx
Jesse Wichmann
Jesús R. Cantú
Jim Baltaxe
Jim Martin
Jim Rittenhouse
Joey Groah
john
John Broglia
JOHN J LEVANDUSKI
John L Vogt
John Lamar
John Muth

ohnny Gonzakes
on Jebus!
onathan Rodriguez
onny Hinkle
oost
osh Parr
osh Rosenbaum
oshua Bowers
uan Carlos Rodríguez García
ustin Gray
ap
athryn Berghold
eith Bufkin
en Nickerson
enneth A. Brown
enneth Leyden
evin Cuffe
evin Rubin
izer Nix
ris Kulin
urt 'KC' Christenson
urt Prünner
yle Clayton Aukland
aura Ivers
eon
evid José de Jesús Montes Sánchez
ina van Brügge
ogan Naugle
ogan Rodgers
ucy Sousa
uis Vives
uke Wisely
. Struik
arc Mason
arc Reiner
ark Haven Britt
ark Netter
ark Patterson
ark Sasaki
ark Schmidt
att kund
att LaRock
att Osborne
atthew Crowe
atthew Shaw
atthew Wang
egan & Z Krick
ichael Frizell
ichael Niosi
ichael Walko
ichelle Marsh
ike Scigliano
ike Thurlow
ikel Muxika
Molly Schofield and
Louis Pryor
N.P.
Nasser Rabadi
Nikita Hellsing
Norbert Martin
Nordee
Norman Miles
OH Comics!
Olivier Trottier
Omar Spahi
Ominous Press
One-Quest.com
Pat Shand
Patrick McHugh
paul clark
paul d jarman
Paul Knight
Paul Linchuang
Paul McErlean
Paul Spence
Paul Villarreal
pbear
Philip R. Burns
pund
Raul Ramirez
Ray Woo
Rayhne Sinclair
Rebecca Fraser
Ricardo Sanchez
Richard Foster
Rick Jacobs
Rico Robinson
Robert Alvord
Robert L. Vaughn
Rod Freund
Rodger Chevy Barkus
Roman
Ron Peterson
Ryan Lenig
Ryan Prettyman
Salvador Raga
Samuel Shuskey
Scott C
Scott Morrison
SCOTT W SCHUMACK
Sean Bodnar
Sean Jenkins
Sergey Anikushin
Shintaro Sasaki
Sid Sondergard
Simon Birks
Simon-Pierre Marion
simalarkey
Souhail Khoury
Space Goat Productions, Inc.
Spencer Clawson
Stacy Horesh
Stephen B
Steve Franceschi
Steven Callen
Steven Hoveke
Steven Latour
Steven Tsai
Steven Vincelli
Stuart Stilborn
Susanna
SwordFire
Sytse Algera
Tai Chan
ted contreras
TexasJV4
Thomas Gernert
Tiberio Velasquez
Tim
Tim Chang
Timothy Connolly
Todd Erwin
Tom Akel
Tony Anjo
Tony Di Schino
Tracy Vierra
Travis Jones
Trent Sessoms
Trisha Wolfe
Try Keeping Up
Tyche
Tyler Sexson
Tyler Trent
Valerie H
vivek goel
Wally Flores Jr
Walt Robillard
Wayne Robbins
Wendy Cheairs
Yaroslava Goncharova

MAKEUP GOLGOTHA PAGE

Sorry we missed you there!

Bobby Torres
Jack Bentele
Brian Laliberte
Michael Ciccone
Irene Swesey
Mike Ohsfeldt
Jason Beltram
Marcus A.
Chiedozie Ukachukwu
David J Kehoe
Andrew Abarca
Owen Crabtree
Marlon Mitchell
Jim Heron
Jeff Short
Charles Crapo
Brian Flinn
Charlie McElvy
Doug Wagner
GeorgeZ
Staggeron
Frankie
Mike Montgomery
Jen S.
Adrian Martinez II
Sonya Park
John Dodds

SPECIAL PREVIEW

BY
MATT HAWKINS & RAFFAELE IENCO

My brother Matthew died five years ago today.

I want it to be the robots' fault, but it's not.

It was mine.

The Pacifiers tried to help him.
SORRY.
HEY!
CITIZEN, PLEASE SLOW DOWN. DO NOT INJURE YOURSELF...
...OR SOMEONE ELSE.

Everything I did, everything I will do, was for Maricela.
Because I love her.
And love is impossible here.

I had no idea it would change everything.
CITIZEN MATTHEW, WE WANT TO HELP YOU.

Everything was perfect before.
PLEASE STOP.
FOR YOUR OWN PROTECTION.

No violence.

No sickness.
WHUMP

No pain.
I DON'T WANT YOUR HELP.

Matthew was two years older than me.

He always watched out for me.

AHH
THUNK

NO!

He died so that Maricela and I could escape.
AHHH

WHAM

CITIZENS, WE DO NOT WISH TO DISRUPT YOUR HARMONY.
THIS MIGHT BE DISTURBING TO YOU, PLEASE GO ABOUT YOUR DAY.
THERE'S FRESH ICE CREAM IN THE CAFETERIA.

AIRLIFT INCOMING NINETY SECONDS.
HE'LL BE DEAD IN THIRTY-SEVEN SECONDS.
WHY DID YOU RUN, CITIZEN?

WHY...WHY WERE WE NEVER TOLD THE TRUTH?

Twenty-three years ago I was born a sexless baby like everyone else.
CHILDBIRTH IS A SIMPLE PROCESS, CITIZEN; THERE WILL BE NO PAIN.

PUSH NOW.

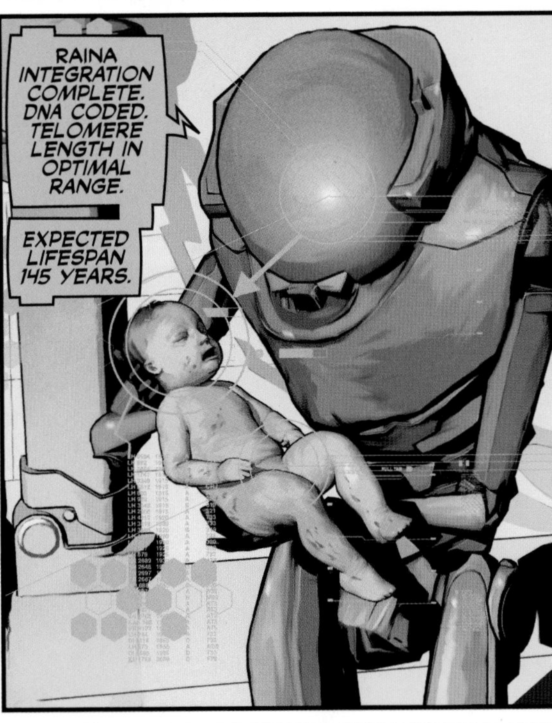
RAINA INTEGRATION COMPLETE. DNA CODED. TELOMERE LENGTH IN OPTIMAL RANGE.
EXPECTED LIFESPAN 145 YEARS.

I don't remember my mother.
IT'S IMPORTANT FOR EMOTIONAL STABILITY THAT YOU PHYSICALLY TOUCH IT IN THE FIRST TWO YEARS. ITS RAINA WILL COMMUNICATE WITH YOURS WHEN IT NEEDS ATTENTION.

Relationships were purely for reproductive purposes. It was rare for a couple to be together more than ten years.

At age three I was taken to a communal educational facility and permanently separated from my parents.
Everyone was taught the same way, the same things. Diversity was forbidden.

WHAT IS THIS?
A CUBE.

WHAT ABOUT THE FOURTH THROUGH SIXTH DIMENSIONS?
TESSERACT, PENTERACT AND SEXTERACT.
WHAT IS THE LESSON?
PERSPECTIVE IS MISLEADING AND DAMAGING TO THE COMMUNITY.

Like all the kids, my best friend and surrogate parent was RAINA.
My RAINA.

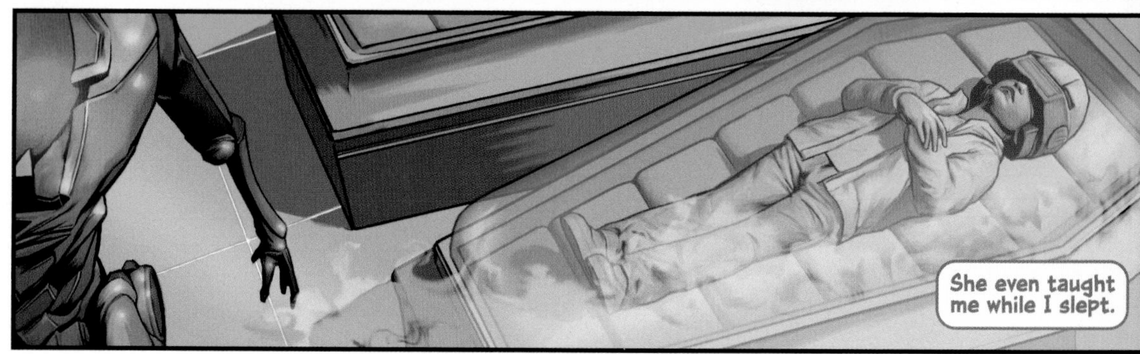
She even taught me while I slept.

The Choosing.
On our thirteenth year we become Citizens. We choose our gender.
We choose our name.
CONGRATULATIONS, CHILDREN.
YOU'VE DONE WELL ON YOUR JOURNEY TO BECOMING ONE WITH THE REST OF US.
BEFORE WE CHOOSE, LET US REMEMBER THE FOUR PILLARS.
COMMUNITY. PEACE. HARMONY. EQUALITY.

When it was my turn I knew what I wanted.

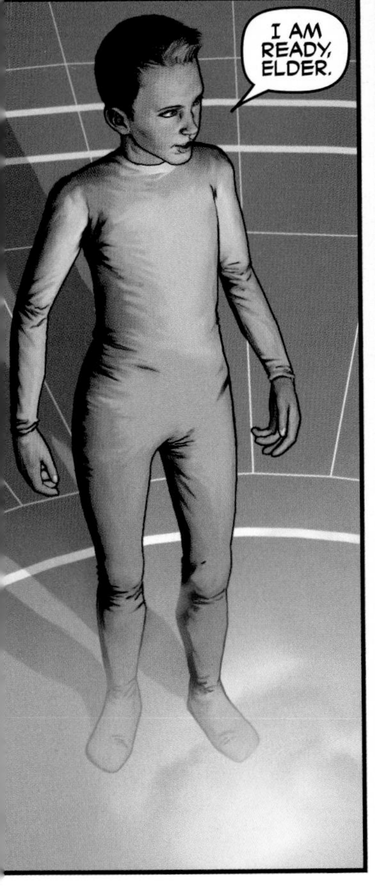
I AM READY, ELDER.

AND HOW DO YOU CHOOSE?

I wanted to be like my older brother MATTHEW.
MALE AND WOULD LIKE TO BE CALLED MICHAEL.

At eighteen I moved into communal building 37-G.
YOU'RE AN ADULT NOW.
IT'S GOING TO SEEM WEIRD AT FIRST TO SLEEP IN A ROOM BY YOURSELF, BUT YOU'LL GET USED TO IT.
HERE'S YOUR NEW HOME.
IT LOOKS LIKE YOURS.
THEY'RE ALL THE SAME.
THE CAFETERIA IS ALWAYS OPEN AND HAS SNACKS, BUT MEALS ARE SERVED AT YOUR SCHEDULED TIME.
ARE YOU STILL UNDER CONTRACT WITH MICHELLE?
NAH, SHE AND I DECIDED NOT TO RENEW AFTER THE ONE-YEAR COMMITMENT ENDED.
ON THAT SUBJECT, YOU CAN'T HAVE SEX IN YOUR UNIT; YOU'LL NEED TO USE ONE OF THE ROOMS ON THE SECOND FLOOR FOR THAT.
THANKS, MATTHEW. I'LL SEE YOU LATER?
DEFINITELY. YOU'LL BE FINE, MICHAEL, JUST TRUST YOUR *RAINA.* SHE'LL KEEP YOU ON THE RIGHT PATH.

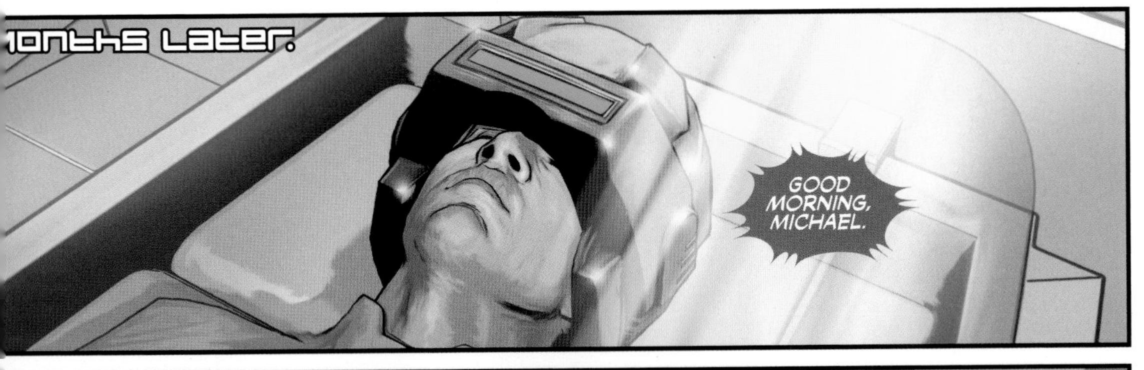
ONTHS LATER.
GOOD MORNING, MICHAEL.

GOOD MORNING, RAINA.
YOUR CORTISOL LEVELS ARE ELEVATED. HOW ARE YOU FEELING?

I'M FINE... EXCITED FOR THE TRIP. I'VE NEVER BEEN OUT OF THE CITY.
WERE YOU ABLE TO GET ME INTO ASTRONOMY? WOLF CREEK HAS THE BEST VIEWS AND I WANT TO KNOW WHAT I'M LOOKING AT.
YES, YOU HAVE THAT AT 1100 AND PLYOMETRICS AT 1600 AND DINNER WITH MATTHEW AND THOMAS AT 1900 IN BUILDING 35-A.

DO YOU THINK WOLF CREEK WILL BE FUN?
YES, OF COURSE, IT'S A PARADISE AND THERE'S SO MUCH TO DO THERE. YOU DREAMED ABOUT IT AGAIN LAST NIGHT. WOULD YOU LIKE TO WATCH PLAYBACK?

SURE!

WOW.
YOU'RE GOING TO HAVE AN EXPERIENCE YOU'LL NEVER FORGET.

I had signed up with Matthew and his friend Thomas for Wolf Creek. We lived near the ocean so a mountain resort seemed fun.
We were encouraged to spend sixteen weeks a year in the resorts.
They were designed to facilitate community fellowship and foster a kinship with the natural world.
THIS IS THOMAS, HE LIVES IN 35-A.
NICE TO MEET YOU. LET ME KNOW IF I CAN DO ANYTHING TO MAKE YOUR TRIP MORE MEMORABLE.
THANKS, REBECCA, WAS IT?
YEAH, I'LL SEE YOU LATER.
THANKS FOR THE INTRO; MY RAINA SCORES HER WITH A HIGH COMPATIBILITY FACTOR.
CITIZEN, EXCUSE ME!
THAT DRINK IS NOT OPTIMIZED FOR YOUR NUTRITIONAL NEEDS.
THIS ONE IS. LABELING ERROR. MY APOLOGIES, CITIZEN.
WE'VE RESERVED A CAMPFIRE FOR THE THIRD NIGHT.
I'D LIKE TO INVITE HER IF THAT'S OKAY WITH EVERYONE.

It took four hours to get there and we had a nice view of the countryside.
Suborbital would have taken fifteen minutes, but back then I had no concept of the value of time. I didn't understand what it meant to hurry.

I wish I could make everything the way it used to be.

It was better. We lived long lives of leisure and happiness.

But love and independence are incompatible to that world. Once tasted, they're impossible to repress.

WOLF CREEK MOUNTAIN

THERE'S A ONE-HOUR ORIENTATION MEETING AND TOUR OF THE FACILITIES.
THERE'S A ONE HOUR ORIENTATION MEETING AND TOUR OF THE FACILITIES.
FEEL THAT AIR?
ONE THOUSAND SIX HUNDRED METER ELEVATION. THE AIR IS THINNER HERE.

THIS MEETING WITH THE EASTERNERS SHOULD LAST MAYBE TWO HOURS; I'D LIKE TO RETURN TONIGHT.
I WILL ARRANGE RETURN TRANSPORT FOR YOUR GROUP AFTER DINNER.
ELDERS, YOUR PARTY AWAITS YOU IN THE WEST CONFERENCE ROOM.

WELCOME TO WOLF CREEK.
AN UPDATED CALENDAR OF EVENTS IS BEING SYNCED. SOME EVENTS FILL QUICKLY SO SIGN UP AS SOON AS POSSIBLE.

MATTHEW WANTS YOU TO JOIN HIM.
TELL HIM I'LL BE THERE IN A BIT.
I CAN SEE ONE OF THE TOWERS FROM HERE.
TELL ME ABOUT IT.
THE ONE YOU'RE LOOKING AT WAS CONSTRUCTED OVER SEVEN HUNDRED YEARS AGO.
IT'S TWO HUNDRED KILOMETERS TALL AND AT ITS APEX ARE VAST SOLAR ARRAYS EXTENDED TO CAPTURE SOLAR ENERGY AND TRANSFER IT BACK TO THE SURFACE FOR ALL OUR ENERGY NEEDS.

What's the one thing a perfectly engineered and ordered society can't control?
Mother Nature.
MATTHEW IS INSISTENT YOU COME NOW. THERE'S AN ELDER ABOUT TO LEAVE ON AN INCOMING TRANSPORT THAT WANTS TO SPEAK WITH YOU.
OH OKAY, TELL HIM I'LL BE RIGHT THERE.
CAN YOU RESERVE MORE TIME ON THIS TELESCOPE TOMORROW NIGHT?
NO OPENINGS TOMORROW. BUT SAME TIME IS AVAILABLE THE FOLLOWING NIGHT. DO YOU WANT THAT?
YES, PLEASE.

A dark age
was about
to return.

Nothing
would ever
be the
same.

THERE HE IS.
HEY, BUDDY, I WANT YOU TO MEET ELDER SHARON.
HELLO, MICHAEL, I'D LIKE TO INTRODUCE YOU AND MATTHEW TO SOME YOUNG LADIES. YOU'RE BOTH APPROACHING THE OPTIMAL FERTILITY AGE. IT'S YOUR DUTY TO REPRODUCE, AFTER ALL.
KKRASH!!
I found out later it was an electromagnetic pulse. It wiped out everything.
And in an instant, in the blinking of an eye...

...the world I knew was gone.

Before that day, I'd never seen a person suffer.
Never witnessed violence.

I'd never seen anyone die.

Death is a constant companion now.

And there's no going back.

The Top Cow essentials checklist: